Kissing
MY BEST FRIEND'S BROTHER AGAIN

HEAVEN J. FOX

DEDICATION

To all the readers who love
Kissing Cousins
&
Kissing My Best Friend's Brother.

.

ACKNOWLEDGMENTS

Thank you Lord, for giving me this gift in a way that can entertain and benefit others.

Thanks to my family for being so supportive and inspirational.

Thanks to you! My readers who keep me motivated by your awesome reviews!

.

CHAPTER 1
NYLA

The first day going back to school was the worst. Aside from not wanting to be here at all, I didn't want to hear what people were saying about me behind my back. I knew people were going to be looking at me strange either about the abortion or the incident with, Jax.

I just don't understand why my mom couldn't just let me go live with my dad or homeschool me. Doesn't she realize that my life could be in danger? Jax is a fool. A crazy one at that.

I passed, Gia and Levi in the hallway on the way to my locker. I heard, Gia calling my name but

I acted like I didn't. Levi knew better than to utter my name.

I gathered my books and headed to first period but of course, Gia caught me at the door. "Hey! What's up? I was calling you but you walked right past." I didn't say a word I just look at her and then looked away. "Well, I guess you still don't want to talk to me." *No shit Sherlock you must be a genius.* Of course, I didn't want to talk to her or anyone.

"Are you ever going to talk to us again?" I shrug my shoulders and walk into class. "Fine, then."

I felt bad treating her that way but I just wasn't in the mood to talk. What was there to talk about anyway? Nothing but, Jax or Levi.

I couldn't concentrate in any of my classes. I felt like today was just a big waste. I had a test in Honors Biology that I knew nothing about. I'm pretty sure that was a big fat F. I tried to buy some time by explaining to the teacher to let me take the test at a later date, but no such luck. I told her my days missed wasn't my fault because I was sick, but of course, she didn't want to hear it. I certainly wasn't going to tell her the truth. I tried to get missing assignments from my classes but the teacher said it was my responsibility to find out what I missed and to turn it in. *Isn't that what I was trying to do?* But I suppose I'm supposed to ask another student.

I raise my hand to get the teacher's attention. She answers me with a sigh like I was irritating her. "May I use the restroom?" I ask her. She rolls her eyes and point me in the direction of the hall pass. I return the eye roll.

I didn't have to use the bathroom, I just wanted to get out of class. I walk as slow as I could toward the restroom because I wasn't trying to get back to class anytime soon.

The hair on the back of my neck stands and before I had time to react, I'm being pulled backward into a storage closet.

"So, what's up? Why you been ignoring me? You don't love me no more or something?"

My mouth flew open as the blood running through my veins felt like hot lava and again I was stuck and unable to move as I stared into, Jax's face.

CHAPTER 2
LEVI

T he bell rung and I was probably the happiest man walking the halls on the way to lunch because my stomach was growling up something fierce. I didn't care what was on the menu today; I was going to eat it and not complain.

"What's up?" Camila stopped me in the hallway. I greeted her with the anticipation that I wanted to hurry up with the pleasantries and get some food into my belly. "Have you seen, Nyla?

What kind of question was that? "Nah, you see her and talk to her more than me these days." I couldn't help but show the dampened mood on my face.

"I'm sure she'll get over being mad at you soon. She's just dealing with a lot right now."

I had to take a double look at, Camila because I couldn't believe something that nice was coming out of her mouth. "I don't know about that. Maybe it was best if I would have just stayed out of it," I shrug.

"You did the right thing. Don't let it beat you up too bad," she said with a raised eyebrow. "Anyway, one of her little friends gave me her book bag and stuff saying she went to the bathroom in the middle of class and never came back."

My mouth twists to the side as my mind searches for a reason for, Nyla to do that. "I don't know. Maybe check the girls' bathroom and make sure she's okay."

"That's the thing. I did that already, and she wasn't in any of them." All of a sudden, her shoulders go limp, and a frown covers her face. "I think I have a feeling of where she might be."

I was going to just let, Camila finish the search on her own but the look she gave sent butterflies through my stomach and not the good kind. I ran to catch up to her, and she stopped at the storage room door and dropped the things she was carrying to the floor. As she swung the door open I just   about   lost   it.

CHAPTER 3
NYLA

W e were in the cafeteria and, Jax kept trying to buy me something to eat. I kept telling him I wanted nothing from him but you know how persistent he can be.

"Is this better? We're in a room full of people so you know I'm not going to do anything to you, baby."

Even with that being the case just being in his presence was enough to shoot my nerves through the roof. "I-I'm not hungry." There was no way I was going to eat lunch with him. This guy has got to be loony.

"Look, I just needed to talk to you. I thought going into the storage room would give us some privacy, but you were acting like I was about to kill you or something." He laughed at my fear of him as if it were some big joke.

"Sit down," he orders me.

I couldn't even if I wanted to which I didn't. I rub my arm looking for someone to rescue me in a bustling room full of people. Everyone was going on about their business as if me and, Jax were a normal thing. My mind was crying out for help and no one heard me.

"Sit down!" He grabs me by my arm and yanks me downward.

"I-I need to get my stuff from the last class I was in," I said looking for a way out with the truth.

"Your stuff ain't going nowhere, Shawty." He pushes the lunch he bought me closer. "Eat," he demands.

I pick up a half fry, place it into my mouth and chew slowly. No matter how hard I try to swallow, the fry did not want to go down.

"Look, I'm sorry about what went down before."

Did he really think those words would erase the horrific thing he did to me? Did he think I would forgive him for that and say it's okay?

"That's just me, you know? I kinda like it rough... it's exciting in the heat of the moment."

My face contorts into disgust, "Exciting! What's exciting about rape?" I couldn't hold my silence any longer.

"Shhhhh!" He held his finger to his lip. "Why the hell you so loud?" He scoots his chair closer to me and my anger exchanges with fear again. "Most girls like it rough."

"No girl likes to be raped, Jax!" Tears were

forming in my eyes ready to fall to the surface.

He rolls his eyes, "I really wish you would stop saying that." He stuffs the rest of his burger into his mouth and takes a sip of his drink before chewing. "I didn't rape you, Nyla. I forget how young you are sometimes."

"Young has nothing to do with it. You held a gun to me, Jax!"

"You act like I held a gun to your head while we were having sex!" His face scrunches as his anger submerges. "If I had handcuffs, I would have cuffed you to a tree... now that would have been bangin'!" He grins as if that was something I'd find interesting.

Vomit climbs the back of my throat and I fight hard to keep it down. "I-I can't do this." I don't even understand why he's talking to me.

"Okay, if you're not hungry you don't have to eat." He moves my tray back and scoots me closer to him so we're face to face. My cringe is worse than the doctor trying to give me a shot and I am scared to death of needles. "Communication is key to a great relationship. Now I know you don't like it rough so next time I'll be gentle." His grin is like the Joker from Batman.

"There won't be a next time!" I scream trying to draw attention our way. Now I know exactly what's he's doing. Why he's trying his hardest to play nice. "I'm not dropping the charges, Jax." I say looking him in the eye with confidence.

"Charges? What charges, Nyla?" The emotions on his face shows confusion, but it's a fake emotion, which makes me confused.

"I know you know I filed rape charges against

you."

"Oh, that!" He laughs. "Yea, no... there's no charges, sweetheart. I know you were just in your feelings at the time so I'll let that little bullshit slide."

He's so stupid it makes me sick. "You can try to be nice all you want. You're going down for what you did to me."

"So, you are freaky. I knew it." He laughs again still holding on tightly to my hands not letting them go. "Sure baby, I'll go down on you but you have to return the favor."

I use every source of strength in me to snatch my hands away, "you're disgusting!" I stand up totally done with this conversation.

He stands up too and holds me in a tight hug. My arms remain limp, glued to my sides. "Here's the thing baby, I doubt those papers ever made it to the police station." I look up at him with question marks etched across my face. "The officers that came out to your house, just happened to be my uncle and step-father." He pushes me away at arm's length to get a better look at my reaction. "Ironic, isn't it?"

CHAPTER 4
LEVI

I couldn't believe how hard up, Camila was. She knew the way I felt about, Nyla, especially with everything she has been through. "Are you that desperate?"

"Excuse me?" she places her hands on her hips as she comes out of the supply closet. There was no way I was about to walk in there with her.

"I know you're new to James Taylor but you're not that new. No way am I going in there with you." I shake my head and grind my teeth.

"Oh, you think I'm trying to get with you?" She laughed so hard like the thought was unheard of. "Boy please! To be honest, you're not my type. I mean you're cute an all but the virgin boy attitude is a turnoff for me. Plus, your way younger than me."

Okay, I admit what she said was a blow to my manhood but I agree, she wasn't my type either because she was a little too out there for me. "You're only a grade higher than me."

"Yea, I'd love to stay and debate this with you but as I said before I'm on a mission to find my sister." She took off full speed down the hall again.

I scratched my head and kind of turned around in a circle wondering if I should just go eat before I missed lunch altogether. But then my mind got the best of me wondering if, Camila was seriously worried about, Nyla.

We looked around in a few more empty classrooms, and the boiler room, Nyla was nowhere to be found. "Wait! Why didn't you just call her cell?" All this running around seemed to be nothing but a big waste of time.

"That was the first thing I did, genius," she sighed. "I'm done looking for this girl. I'm starving."

"I've been starving. Let's hurry up and get in line before they close everything down."

When we got to the lunch room, Camila and I stopped dead in our tracks as if it were a force field that stopped us. "Do you see what the hell I'm seeing?" Camila asked me.

I couldn't believe my eyes. Right there in front of me was, Nyla and Jax. Hugging. What. The. Hell.

"Come on, they're closing up shop," Camila said as she ran into the food line.

I couldn't move. I don't even think my stomach

growled because it was too busy doing other things. I stood there for a minute because when their embrace was done, I wanted her to see me see her.

"Are you coming through? Because we're locking everything up in two minutes," the lunch lady said.

As I was about to get something to eat, Nyla started walking in my direction so I made a split decision to forget about eating so I could talk to her.

"Nyla," she ignored me and kept walking. I run to catch up to her and grab her arm so she could face me. "What's up with that?" I gesture in, Jax's direction.

"Nothing. Don't worry about it," she said hardly looking at me.

How could she forgive him for doing what he did to her but can barely look at me? I didn't go after her. I refused to keep trying with her when I know I didn't do anything wrong. I fall back onto the wall feeling defeated. I didn't even get to eat anything fooling around with her.

"Here you go, boss." Camila hands me a slice of pizza and some cold fries. "I figured you weren't going to make it through before they closed down."

"Thanks. I appreciate it."

"I know you do."

CHAPTER 5
NYLA

$\curlywedge$

Mom told me to catch a ride home with, Gia and Levi today. I already knew I wasn't going to do that, but there was no use in arguing the point. Camila stayed after for Cheerleading practice. I wasn't just going to sit there and watch them practice.

It was getting chilly, so I pulled my sweater together and buttoned it. I wish I would have worn my jacket instead.

There were groups of kids walking together from school on each side of the street. I felt like a fool being the only one walking alone. I rarely walk. Our house is a little less than two miles away. My mom hates for me to walk because she says it's not safe for young girls to walk alone. But as long as I beat her home, she'll never know.

I make it to the top of the hill and a car zooms into my path stopping me from crossing the street. "Get in."

I roll my eyes and try to walk around the car but each time he moves the car forward not letting me cross. "What don't you understand, Levi? I want nothing to do with you."

"That's fine, Nyla. I'm so over trying to figure you out. Your mom said I'm supposed to give you a ride home and that's what I'm going to do."

"I don't care what my mom says, I'm not getting in the car with you."

"Oh, but if I were, Jax you'd probably jump in the car with no questions asked, huh?"

His way of thinking made my skin crawl. *How could he even think that? Doesn't he know I'm staying away from him for his own good?* I shake my head and fold my arms trying my hardest not to make a tear fall. I refuse to move. He gets out of the car and walks around to me.

"Nyla, just get in the car. I'm not trying to have your mom ring down her raft on me." I don't move. I don't even look at him. "Look, we don't even have to talk. I don't even care that you don't want to be with me anymore. That's your choice."

I was still mad at him for telling my mom, but my being mad still didn't make me not want him. I wanted him. Badly. But there was nothing I could do about it. Jax made it very clear that if he heard or seen me around, Levi... he'd kill him. I wasn't sure if he was speaking figuratively or literally but I didn't want to find out.

"Come on, please," Levi grabs my arm to move me toward his car, but I shove him away. "Why are you acting like this?" he bends down to look into my face.

"Why can't you just leave me alone!"

"I'm trying, Nyla!" he yells. "Every day I try not to think about you. I want to call you or text you but I don't because I know you wouldn't answer, anyway."

He's right. I wouldn't. But that doesn't mean I wouldn't want to. He holds both of my folded arms in his hands and I can feel pieces of my anger chipping away. "Please." He asks again this time softer. My arms relax a bit but still folded. I'm weighing my options. I don't want to get in trouble with my mom by walking and it is rather a tiring walk. Besides, what are my chances of, Jax seeing me?

"I don't know. I'm still mad at you." I bite down on my teeth to suppress a smile that tries to bogart its way onto my face.

"I know you are." He moves in closer to me. "I wish you weren't though," he says as he holds my face in his hands and kisses my forehead.

I close my eyes wishing he would kiss me like he used to. Just this one last time, and then after... I could go back to hating him. I unfold my arms and wrap them around his waist inviting him to do what I needed.

"I miss you so much, Nyla." He squeezes me tight.

I look up at him, "I miss you too." He's looking down at me, our lips inches apart. I can feel his breath on my face and if I lift up just a bit on my toes, our lips would meet again.

"Can I kiss-" I lift on my toes and meet his lips before he could finish his sentence. I'm melting in his embrace. With each second that passes seems to erase any fear I may be having. "Can we just stop playing games and be together?"

CHAPTER 6
LEVI

I kiss her again before she has a chance to answer. I wanted her to know that no matter what I said a few minutes ago; I wanted her. I wanted her just like this. Why can't we be this way all the time? I won't stop kissing her because I'm afraid to hear her answer.

She pulls away from our kiss and says, "I want to, I really do... but I don't want to be a hypocrite."

"What do you mean?" I ask but I don't let her get too far from me. If I let her out of my arms, she may never come back again.

"I'm not ready to forgive, Gia. I'm still mad as hell at her, which means I can't forgive you either." She tries to free herself from my arms but I won't let her. My heart cries for her and my sister's friendship, but my soul breaks when she includes me.

"Can I ask you a question?" She glances at me expectantly. "How can you forgive him and not me and my sister?" She really tries to break out of my arms now and it takes a little more muscle to not let her loose.

"I definitely didn't forgive him! How would you even think that I would?" She's still trying to break away from me.

"Because, Nyla. I saw you hugging him."

"I wasn't hugging him, Levi! He was making me, kind of like what you're doing now."

My grip on her arms loosen from the thought of her comparing me to, Jax. *How could she do that?* I would never force her to do something she didn't want to do. "It didn't seem like you were putting up much of a fight like you're doing with me."

She reaches back and swings her palm making contact with my face. I keep my head tilted to the side where it landed. The only movement I did was letting her go. I'm staring at the pavement wondering why the hell she has no problem telling me off or hitting me. I bet she's never laid a hand on, Jax.

"Levi, I'm sorry," she apologizes as she tries to look into my face.

I block her hand as she reaches for me. I'm tired of being her punching bag. "Okay, Nyla I hear you."

"I'm dealing with so much stuff right now. Sometimes it's just too much." A tear escapes her eye and I try not to look because I know it will turn my insides to jelly. "He said some stuff to me, Levi. He scares the crap out of me."

My soul groans because her sorrow gets to me and melts all my anger away. She knows I can't resist her especially when she's crying. "What did he say?"

She shakes her head and shuts down when I'm ready to talk about it. "I can't say. All I will say is that he doesn't want me to talk to you or be around you."

"Is he why you shut me off from you?" My anger returns with a vengeance.

"It's not that simple, Levi. If he wasn't in the picture and it could be just me and you without fearing he'd do something to you, I would."

"So, your fear for him is what keeps us apart?" I push her away from me at arm's length. "Your love for me should be stronger than your fear for him."

"My love for you keeps me from you. Why can't you understand that?" She's grabbing on me and I'm trying my best to fight her off because I don't understand what she's talking about. The only thing I get is that fact that she doesn't want to be with me.

"If you don't want to be with me then why are you here?" I'm dying for clarification.

"I'm here because I do love you and want to be with you."

"Then be with me, Nyla!" I grab her and pull her close to me and kiss her. I kiss her as passionately as I could to let her know that *I* will be her protector if she just lets me.

I hear a car pull up alongside us but I don't stop kissing her for nothing. Whoever it is, let them watch because I'm not letting her go again.

"You both must have a death wish!"

The sound of that voice tares, Nyla away from me and I'm for sure I've lost her for good this time.

CHAPTER 7
NYLA

⁓

It took everything I had in me to not release any bodily fluids. I was shaking so bad you might think I was about to go into a convulsion. *I knew I should have just kept walking home.*

Levi jumped in front of me. *No! No! No! Don't do that!* My mind was crying out for, Levi's safety but nothing was coming out of my mouth. It was as if my lips were paralyzed.

"Boy, if you don't remove yourself from in-between me and my daughter, I promise you will need a body bag."

"I-I'm sorry, Mrs. Jackson..."

"Boy, if you sing that damn song again, I will ring your neck!"

"N-N-Nooo... I just wanted to explain."

My mom stands face to face with Levi, "okay, explain." She folds her arms tightly across her chest. "Explain why your tongue was down my daughter's throat when I trusted you to have her home an hour ago."

Levi's mouth fell open but nothing came out. He glanced over at me and mine did the same.

"Uh huh. That's what I thought. From here on out, Mr. Nash you are to not have any contact with my daughter. Do you understand?"

"Mrs. Jackson!" Levi's voice mimicked his shock. "That's a little harsh don't you think?"

"Nod your head and say, *yes Mrs. Jackson, I understand.*" Levi reluctantly did what he was told. "And don't *think* your mother won't be hearing about this!"

Levi leaned against his car with his head down. I wished there was something I could say to make him feel better, but I knew if I said anything to him my mother would blow up. Even though I know she's going to let me have it as soon as we get into the car.

We drove in silence for about a block before she started in on me. "Where the hell is your mind sometimes, Nyla?" I shift in my seat and continue to stare straight out the windshield. "Did you not learn anything from the first time?"

I stay silent because her questions are stupid. I will be seventeen soon, am I not supposed to be having feeling for the opposite sex?

"Where are we going?" I ask when I noticed we were headed in the opposite direction from our house.

"I'm going to the gas station for gas and then back to the school to pick up, Camila." She pauses for a moment. "Do you see how that works?"

"What?"

"The person who asks a question expects an answer in return." I roll my eyes without her knowing.

After getting gas, we sit in the school parking lot waiting on, Camila. My mom presses the button to glide her seat backward. After getting as comfortable as she could, she's now ready to resume her chastisement.

"Nyla. You know I only want what's best for you right?" I'm supposed to say yes or nod my head in agreement but my shoulder wants to hunch itself up and fall back down. "You don't know!" She now reclines the seat back and I'm forced to look at her protruding belly. I know I sound like I hate the baby. I don't. I actually can't wait for it to get here. Then maybe some of the tension will be off me.

"Do you like that boy or something?"

I knew who she was referring to but just to be difficult I say, "who?"

"You know damn well who, Nyla."

No mom, I like kissing boys I don't like! Idiot! If that wasn't the stupidest question I don't know what was. "I guess," I mumble.

"You guess? So, you don't know?"

Is she freaking serious! "Yesssss mom. I likeeeee him!" I bug my eyes at her.

"Humph... I wish I would have known that mess before I had you go stay over there." *I wish too mom, then maybe I wouldn't have even gone to the park to see, Jax.* "How long has this been going on?"

"What do you mean? There's nothing going on."

"You know why all this is happening don't you?" I give her a look that says I have no idea what she was talking about. "You weren't having all this crap happening until you had sex with that, Chase boy."

My mouth flings open. *How did we get here?* "What does, Chase have to do with any of this?"

"Nyla boys sense out the easy girls and that's who they go for to satisfy their boyish desires."

"I sleep with one boy and that makes me easy?" My voices raise a few octaves.

"I'm not saying your easy, I'm saying it looks that way. You've had sex with two boys now and here comes, Levi sniffing around all of a sudden."

"Levi is not sniffing around, mom! And I had consensual sex with one boy the other wasn't my choice!"

My mom rolls her eyes and exhales loudly. "This is just great! All I need is for Daniel to hear about this. He sure called it and here I am sounding like a fool, defending you."

"So! Who cares about, Daniel? He's not my dad!" I turn around and tune her out. I don't want to hear anything else she has to say.

"Oh, and hand me your phone before I forget."

I couldn't help but hear that. "My phone? Why?"

"Because, Nyla... when I say no contact that's exactly what I mean."

And when I say, I hate you... that's exactly what I mean.

CHAPTER 8
LEVI

Why does it feel like whenever, Nyla and I finally have a chance something pulls us further apart? It's like a Merry-Go-Round or a roller coaster with her and not in a fun way.

I can't believe her mother went off on me like that. That is, *one* bugged out lady.

As soon as I walk into the house, my mom goes in on me. "Lee!" she summons me.

I exhale and make a bee-line towards her voice, "Yes, mom."

"What's going on, Lee?"

I scratch my head and say, "she called you already?"

"You know she did. Now what is this I hear about you and, Nyla?"

"Oh my gosh, mom. It was just a kiss."

"Why didn't you tell me? The way, Olivia explains it, it was more than just a kiss."

"That lady is crazy! How could it be more than a kiss when we were outside in the open?"

"Well, I'm sure she was exaggerating. But you know how she is about her daughter especially when you know what happened to her."

"So, what? I'm supposed to not have feelings for the girl because that happened to her?" If anything, it makes me have more feelings for her.

"I don't know, Lee. Just cool things with, Nyla for now. She has a lot of things she needs to sort out in her mind, okay?"

"Okay, mom," I shrug.

I fall back onto my bed replaying the kisses, Nyla and I shared and I want her to be here with me right now. I hope she doesn't think from this incident that I wouldn't be able to protect her. It was her mom, she trumps everything and everyone.

I know her mom said no contact, but I have to text her to let her know I'm thinking about her. *"Hey bae, thinking about u and missing u and ur kisses. I wish u were here right now n my arms. Don't let ur mom get u down. I love u. <heart eyes emoji>"*

I scroll through her pics on Instagram feeling like she's miles away from me even though she's just down the block and around the corner. It's only been about five minutes since I sent the text but its feeling like forever waiting for her to reply.

"Hey." I get a Messenger notification from Nyla. *About time.*

"You okay?"
"I'm fine. I was about to ask u the same thing."
"I'm good. Can't stop thinking about u tho."
"Same here. Sorry about my mom. U no how she can trip."
"It's cool. I'm just glad u not mad at me. I don't know what I would do if I could never feel ur lips on mine again."
"lol! Shut up... never that. I don't care what my mom says... I'm not going to stop seeing u."
"It's kind of hard with ur mom putting u on lockdown."
"Well, we'll just have to skip school."
"<Shocked face emoji, heart eyes emoji>"
"What? Lol It's not like it would be the first time."
"Where u want to go?"
"Hmmm... IDK let's get a room."

My phone slips out of my hands and smacks me in the face. *Dang I hate that!* Is she serious? I stare at her last message for what feels like eternity and I don't know how to respond to that. Does she want to just chill or Netflix and Chill? Can you even get Netflix at a motel?

"Ok, <sunglasses emoji> when?"

I sit up on my bed with the widest nervous grin

etched across my face waiting for her reply.

"NEVER MR NASH! YOU JUST HELPED GET HER CELLPHONE PERMANENTLY TAKEN AND ALL SOCIAL MEDIA DELETED! THANK YOU!"

My heart was about to break through my chest from beating so hard. I drop my phone onto my bed and back away like whoever was on the other end could see me. WTF just happened?

Beads of sweat form on my brow because now I'm paranoid wondering if I were ever talking to, Nyla. *Her mom is freaking crazy! Weird!*

"LEVI!!!"

Oh. My. Gosh. No, this lady did not just call my mom and snitch that fast.

Before I can make it to my bedroom door, my mom burst in faster and harder than a tornado wind pulling open a screen door. "Let me see your phone!" My mom demanded.

I hand it over quickly with no problem because I had nothing to hide. She's nervous and her hands are shaking trying to navigate through my phone. She gives up and shoves it back into my hand. "Pull it up!"

"Pull up what?" I knew what she was talking about, I don't know why I was giving her a hard time. She needed to calm down though because it's not even that serious.

"Pull up the thingy-ma-jiggy on the whatchamacallit."

I cover my mouth with the back of my hand to suppress a smile. It wasn't funny, funny, but it was funny. "Mom, for real calm down, dang." I pull up, Nyla and I's conversation on Messenger and hand her the phone for her to read over.

After a few seconds her mouth hangs open, and she looks up at me. "You were talking about taking this girl to a hotel?"

I roll my eyes playfully. "Motel mom. We were just talking about it. I doubt if we were gonna really do it."

"Lee! What did I just tell you about this girl?"

"This girl? Mom you're acting like, Nyla's a stranger."

"I don't know, Lee. I'm beginning to feel like she is. People change after something traumatic happens to them sometimes. This just isn't like her."

"What isn't like her, mom? Truth be told, we've been liking each other and talking. We just didn't tell you guys." I rub the back of my neck to relieve some tension. "Technically she was my girlfriend when she got raped."

"Lee!" My mom covered her mouth with her hands and wouldn't stop staring at me.

"What? Tell Mrs. Olivia Jackson that."

CHAPTER 9
NYLA

I'm sitting here staring at my laptop and totally regret sending my last message when, Levi doesn't respond.

"Hey, so I've been meaning to ask you, what was up with you and, Jax today?" Camila sits up on her bed while her fingers work overtime on her phone.

"Oh. I dunno, he's crazy." I'm trying to think on what I should tell her, if anything at all. "I left class to go to the bathroom and the next thing I know, he's pulling me into a closet."

Camila's mouth hung open. "He didn't... you know."

"No! But I was so scared thinking he would,

especially after what you told me about him."

She looked relieved. I don't know if it was relief that he didn't hurt me again or relief that nothing happened because she may be into him.

"I knew it! The supply closet was the first place we looked."

"We?"

"Yea, Levi and I," she laughed. "You should have seen his face when nobody was in the closet. This fool really thought I was making it up just to get him to the closet to jump his bones. As if Camila does desperate," she spoke about herself in third person.

I glance at my laptop screen again and my stomach churns when I see, Levi still hasn't responded to my message. "Ugh!" I slap myself on the forehead, "how stupid can I be."

"What's wrong?" Camila asks.

I was about to tell her when I looked at my screen closer. Down at the bottom on the right-hand side, it showed I had no internet connection. That's probably why, Levi's not responding! "Do you have Wi-Fi connection?" I asked Camila.

"Yeah. Maybe restart your computer," Camila suggested.

"What are you doing?" I jump as my mother appeared in the doorway with her hand permanently attached to her bulging belly.

"Uh, homework." I glance at my laptop to make sure any evidence of contact with, Levi wasn't showing.

She walks closer to me. "Give me your laptop, Kindle, and iPad. When I said no contact with that boy, that's exactly what I meant, Nyla."

"I haven't had contact," flew out of my mouth before I had time to think about my answer. "How am I supposed to do my homework and write my papers?"

"Girl, I will slap you three times if you lie to me again! But I forgot, you don't care about what I say because you're not going to stop talking to him." My mom folded her arms and rocked her neck. "And for that you can do things the old-fashioned way. Pens, paper, and the library."

My eyebrows burrow together because I'm wondering how the words I said to, Levi are coming out of her mouth. I glance over at, Camila and she shrugs.

"Oh... and your plans to flick and get a hotel room with that boy will never happen either."

How. Did. She. Know? Did, Levi tell on me again? Why would he do that? I'm so confused right now.

"I blocked all your access to Wi-Fi and any new devices coming in so you can try and be cunning by acquiring another device but it won't work." She walked around my room collecting all my devices with a vengeance. "I clearly told you *and* him... no contact! I can't even get any rest in the next room with your cellphone dinging every few seconds. Imagine my surprise when *my daughter* is the one suggesting flicking and hotel rooms! What the hell is wrong with you? Are you that hot in the ass for attention?"

The words spewing from my mom's mouth stung like my body was lying in a closed casket filled with wasp and blackjacks. "Wow, mom."

"Wow mom, nothing! From now on you will go

to and from school. That is it!" *Oh wow, was that my punishment?*

"Big deal, mom. That's what I do every day!" I raise my voice and I don't care at all.

"It really is," Camila snickers until my mom gives her the death stare.

"I'll just talk to, Levi when I get to school. And if we want to have sex, we can just go into a supply closet, empty classroom, or the basement."

Before I knew it, my mom had smacked me so hard, my head hit the wall.

"Olivia!" Daniel runs into the room and grabs my mom. She hands Daniel all of my electronics and points her finger in my face.

"Be careful of things you wish for because you just might get it sooner than you think."

CHAPTER 10
LEVI

M y emotions were all over the place this morning. I didn't know if I were eager to see, Nyla or if I wanted to avoid her.

I stop, Gia before she gets out the car. "Gigi, I need you to do me a favor."

"What is it?" She glances at me with a side eye.

"I need you to talk to, Nyla for me so I can see what kind of mood she's in before I walk up to her."

"Hecks no! And walk up to her for what? Didn't mommy tell you to stay away from her?

I turn my head sideways and look at my sister. "C'mon now, Gigi. You know that's not happening."

"Well, it needs to happen. I'm done trying to talk to that girl. If she doesn't want to be my friend, then so be it." Gia folds her arms and frown. I knew it hurt my sister that her best friend was treating her that way.

"How about the three of us sit together at lunch and talk all of this out?"

"I've tried talking to her, Lee... many times. I'm not going to have her continue to crush my spirt because she's dealing with some messed up issues." Gia's eyes were beginning to water. "It's real messed up that she blames me for what happened to her. I'm the shoulder she should lean on but she shuns me instead. I'm done with it."

Gia gets out of the car and slams the door. I guess I'm on my own where, Nyla's concerned.

Since I got here a little early, I went to breakfast to grab a donut and orange juice. When I got there, Nyla was sitting at a table alone with her face buried into a textbook.

"Is this seat taken?" I decided to go with a cheesy pickup line to lighten the mood. It was hard not knowing what really went on last night because I hadn't heard from her.

"Actually, it is," she said.

Somehow, I wasn't expecting that response. "Oooh kay..." I glanced around the cafeteria wondering where I could lick my wounds.

"I'm saving this seat for my boyfriend." I turned to walk away and then she stops me. "Levi if you don't sit down," she laughs.

"About last night..." I hesitate for a moment.

"Yeah, I know. Crazy, right?"

I nod my head. "So, who exactly was I

messaging? You or your mom?"

"Me of course, why would you think it was my mom?" I take out my phone and show her the message. "You have got to be kidding me! She's certified crazy."

"So, what are we going to do? It was hard for you to get out of the house before, now it's just going to be impossible.

"I meant what I said, Levi. We should get a room."

"Y-You were serious about that?"

"Yeah, unless you're not," she says glancing up at me.

"When do you think we should do this?" I suddenly get nervous anticipating our plans. Could we really pull this off?

"I dunno, it's up to you." She hesitates for a moment. "What about now?"

My juice goes down the wrong way and I start choking uncontrollably. After a few minutes of feeling like I was going to choke to death, I say, "What about your mom? She's watching you like a hawk now even more so."

She frowns and her whole mood changes. "If you don't want to go, why don't you just say no."

"No, it's not that..." I don't get to finish my complete thought because the bell rings and she's already gathered her things heading out of the cafeteria.

I run to catch up, "Let's go now."

CHAPTER 11
NYLA & LEVI

$\backsim\!\!\!\supset$

L^{*EVI*}   I go to pay for the motel room and I have no idea what this cost. I'm nervous and shaking. I don't know if you have to be a certain age or if this guy will call the cops on me because I'm underage and should be in school right now, or what.

I'm looking around for a door to walk into and there is none. "Yeah." I hear someone say followed by a lot of coughing and hacking.

There's a guy standing behind a window. I'm guessing now I was supposed to drive up. We've stayed in a few hotels when we used to go on family vacations, before mom... you know. Anyway, I've never seen anything quite like this. "Uh..." I look back at, Nyla sitting there in car and I'm having second thoughts until she waves and smiles. "I need to get a room."

"No shit. And here I was thinking you came for the five-star restaurant." I glance around and didn't see any restaurant around. Smokestack thought I was hilarious. "First time, huh?" He says leaning closer to the window.

"I ain't talking about here, Sunshine," he says laughing and coughing at the same time.

"How much for the room?" He was irritating the hell out of me.

"Twenty-dollars for six hours, fella." I hand him the money and we do a stare off while I'm waiting for the key. "ID," he says like I'm supposed to know.

I hand him my ID in exchange for a key with a big green key chain that has the number twenty-one etched in gold. I'm still standing there feeling awkward as hell waiting for him to give me back my ID.

"Go straight back on your right."

"Uh, my ID, sir?"

"You'll get that back when you return my damn key."

Ohhhh kay.

I scratch my head and hesitantly walk back to the car. As we pull up to number twenty-one, I just sit there and stare.

"You okay?" Nyla asks.

"Yeah, you?"

"Yeah," she giggles. "Are we gonna go in or did

you just have enough to park?" She laughs. I smirk. It was funny but my nerves were taking the fun out of me.

I drum my fingers on the dashboard nervously. Of course, if I were going to lose my virginity I wouldn't want it to be with nobody but, Nyla. Maybe it would be different if she were a virgin too. I guess I'm worried that I won't measure up.

A knock on the window startles me and I jump. I look up and its, Nyla laughing. She opens my door and pulls on my arm. "Why are you acting so scary? It's not like we're going to have sex, Levi."

We're not? You would think her saying that would have calmed my nerves but it downed my mood now. Not that it's a big deal we're not.

"Levi!"

Nyla's already standing in the room with the door open. When the hell did she snatch the key out of my hand? I need to snap out of it. I run in and give her a bear hug lifting her off her feet.

"Levi! You're squeezing me!" She laughs.

"I know. That's the whole point."

NYLA

I place my purse on the end table in the living room section and survey my surrounding. This place wasn't that bad, but it wasn't that great either. I don't know what's up with, Levi. He's seeming more nervous than me right now.

"So, what should we do?" He asks me.

"I dunno. There's a TV. You want to watch something."

"Yeah," he smiles.

I go to the bathroom and when I come out his eyes are bugged out of his head. "What's wrong? Did you see a bug or something?"

"Uh, no. But I don't think you want to watch TV."

"Why not?" I take the remote from him and scoot close to him on the bed.

"T-They have like two channels and it's all..."

Too late. I had already turned the TV on and it was nothing. But. Porn. That was weird. We both felt so awkward now. Maybe even a little embarrassed for some reason.

"So, what now?"

"I dunno."

We literally sat there in silence for ten whole minutes. Not to sound like a whore or that I was hot in the ass, as my mother would say, but I wanted so bad to make out with him. No way was I going to look like a tramp and make the first move, but I was getting annoyed just sitting here. I mean I may get caught or in trouble for this, and if so, I wanted it to count for something.

I take off my shoes and lounge back onto the bed. "I wish I had my phone."

"I know babe," He says removing his shoes and lying beside me. He puts his arm around me waist, snuggling up close to me. *About time!*

"I miss lying beside you," he says in a soft tone. "I wish you were still staying with us."

"Me too." I turn my head towards him and look into his eyes and he reaches over and kiss me. I love this dude so much. In a matter of minutes, the intensity in our kisses grow as he gets on top of me. My breathing heaves in and out at a fast pace but it's not the passion anymore. It's my mind thinking about, Jax and that night. I want to push, Levi off so the thought of, Jax can go away.

"What's wrong?" Levi leans to the side of me taking his weight and the thoughts of, Jax with him.

"Nothing." I flip, Levi over and get on top of him instead and thoughts of, Jax is nowhere to be found and I'm loving it because I'm loving, Levi.

Hating to pull my lips away from, Levi I lift up so he can pull my shirt off and he does the same. Our lips reunite again as he fumbles with my bra and me with his pants.

"Are we really going to do this? I thought you said no sex." He says without taking his lips from mine.

"Shut up," I say.

We're both completely naked and under the cover not sure if we're both comfortable yet with showing each other our body parts but definitely sure we're ready to become one.

He flips me over onto my back and gets on top of me again and I fight from freaking out. I refuse to let, Jax still this moment from me. It was easier when I was on top but I have to still remember that this is his first time and I have to make sure he's comfortable and confident too.

*L*EVI

I'm right here at the entrance ready to go in and I don't. Instead I'm propped up on my hands and my arms are wobbling from being nervous. I'm not nervous about doing it at all. I'm nervous because that last time she had sex with someone was traumatic for her. I don't know if I will hurt her or freak her out. I don't know how to proceed.

"Nyla, I love you so much," I say.

She grabs my face. *She's the only one who could ever do that.* "I love you too," she says back.

I feel a tingle all over my body when she runs her hands down my back and stops on my ass. As I reach down to kiss her again, she pulls me inside her. *Shit!*

Shit. Shit. Shit!!!

Somehow, she's engulfed in my arms and the way she sounds when she moans finishes me. *Damn.* I lay there on top of her. Breathless. Unable to move. Not wanting to move. *Ever.*

Then it hit me like a ton of bricks. I barely got two pumps in. She's going to hate me. Girls like guys who can go for hours, right? I didn't even last two minutes.

I remove my arms from around her and try to sit up but she holds on tight, not letting me go.

"Don't move," she moans. The way she moans makes me grow instantly inside her. I kiss her and then I knew it wasn't over. It was far from over. This time I would be sure to make it last.

N*YLA*

I have never in my life felt something like this. Chase could never hold a candle to, Levi, and this was his first time.

"You lied," I lay back with the cover pulled over

me trying to find my breath again.

"About what?" He glances over at me seriously.

"You said you were a virgin. I couldn't tell?" I smile at him.

"Psh. Yea right. I know you hated me the first time. I didn't even last a minute." He chuckles a bit but I sense he was looking for affirmation.

"Truth?"

"Always."

"I think I... you know. The same time you did." I couldn't help but feel shy. Certain words I wasn't comfortable saying.

He leans on his arm facing me. "What do you mean, think?"

"Because, I've never... before, but I'm pretty sure that's what it was." Thinking about it sent chills radiating down my body. "I've never had sex I've enjoyed before."

"So that first guy you were with..."

"Never."

He lays onto his back with a big grin on his face. "So, I guess you can say we were technically each other's first today, huh?"

"Yup." I liked the sound of that. I move over and lay on, Levi's chest.

"We've got a little more time before we have to be back before your mom picks you up."

"Don't tell me you want another go?"

"I can honestly say you've worn me out."

***

I can't believe how good everything worked out. I'm sitting here on the bench waiting for my mom to pull up and, Levi won't leave.

"Boy go before my mom comes and see you here with me!" I smack his arm playfully.

"I'm trying, but I can't." He puts his arms around me. "I can't help it. It's your fault."

"How is it my fault?"

"Because you got me whipped now, girl."

"Shut up!" He kisses my forehead. I look and can tell my mom's car approaching in the distance. "Levi! She's coming!"

He presses his lips to mine giving me a quick but heartfelt kiss and hauls ass in the opposite direction. "Nyla, I love you!" He yells.

CHAPTER 12
NYLA

T he next day, I grab everything I need for my morning classes because I won't be by this way again until after lunch.

When I close my locker, Jax is standing right in front of me. "How was your day yesterday? You and a certain somebody seemed to be MIA." He's grinning at me trying to intimidate me and feed off my fear. I know now that's what he does and I'm just about sick and tired of it. I refuse to do this anymore.

"Leave me alone!" I shout not caring who heard. I hope everyone did.

I try to walk past him but he grabs my arm. "Who the hell do you think you're talking to?" He squeezes tighter and clinches his jaw.

Inside the anger boils in my veins. I yank my arm back from him, hard. "You must be an idiot if you don't know I'm talking to you." I fold my arms across my chest. My heart is beating out of control and my legs wobble so I shift all my weight to one leg to steady them.

He holds his head back and laughs like I was some big joke. "Look at you! Tryin' to jump all bad." Matt yells his name from down the hall. He comes closer and whispers, "you must think I'm playin' with you. I meant what I said about you not talkin' to dude." He grabs my chin forcefully and pulls it upward so I'd had no choice but to look up at him. "I'ma show you just how good I keep my word."

Matt comes over and gives Jax a fist bump and I high-tail it down the hall towards my class as fast as I could and bump into, Levi.

"Whoa, baby what's wrong?" Levi stops me and asks.

I was trying to play big and bad with, Jax hoping he would leave me alone but it seemed to have backfired and now I was a nervous wreck. "Maybe we should just keep our distance." I look nervously behind him hoping that, Jax wasn't anywhere lurking around.

"What are you talking about?" Levi asked. "All I could think about was you all night. And now you're acting like yesterday never happened."

"I have to get to class, Levi!" My legs still wobbly.

Levi turns around and sees the same person I was looking at. "What did he say to you, Nyla?

You're shaking so bad you look like you're about to fall over."

"He doesn't want me talking to you!"

Levi exhaled loudly and ran his fingers over his head. "I'm getting sick and tired of everyone in my business!" He tries to look into my eyes and I turn away. "Are you seriously thinking about listening to him? Hell no! You mine!"

As weird as it may seem, I think I was more scared of, Jax than I was of my own mother. "I'm trying to spare your life! You may not be scared of him but I am. He hurt me. Not you! Every day I come to school I have full blown panic attacks because I know he's going to be here! Do you know what the feels like every single day?"

He didn't say anything. He just remained silent staring at me. "I have to go," I said heading to homeroom.

On my way to third period it was a lot of commotion coming from down one of the hallways. People were running and jumping over one another trying to get to where the action was. I on the other hand was glad that my next class was in the opposite direction.

My mom always said, *"whenever you see people running to danger, make sure you run in the other direction away from it."* So that's what I was doing.

Some stupid guy bumped into me knocking my book bag from my shoulders. "Fight! Fight!" He yelled throughout the hall not even bother to say 'excuse me' or 'sorry.'

I shake my head at boys' enthusiasm to watch a chick fight. Every teacher seemed to be out of their classrooms to help break up the fight. Mostly the male teachers. The women seemed to try and deter other students from entering the brawl arena and get to their designated classrooms. Some of the kids try to be slick and tell the teacher that their classroom was down that way. She then directed them to go into another classroom nearby and wait there.

I'm pretty sure whatever the fight was about, it had to be over one guy who was playing them both.

I walk into my third period class and it was just about empty except for the nerds. I make it to my seat and sit down. I wondered, if they're here and I'm here what does that make me? Not that being a nerd was a bad thing because it wasn't. I just never thought about myself in any high school category before.

I look on the clock on the wall and we've been sitting here for the last ten minutes teacher-less. Just as soon as that thought enters my mind, the room fills with rowdy rambunctious kids.

"Oh man! Did y'all see that!?" One boy says as he holds his fist to his mouth.

"They were going at it!" Another guy shouted.

I roll my eyes at the simple fact about how guys get off on watching a chick fight. I wonder if they would have the same enthusiasm if it were on pay-per-view and they had to spend money on it. Boys are so stupid. Who knows? They probably would.

"That fight was definitely better than Mayweather vs. McGregor. I know something's got to be broken. Did you see how dude slammed him on his head?"

The other guy cringes, "Ew! I know man. I was fo sho dude broke his neck!"

Dude? It was dudes fighting and not chicks? My stomach falls like I was on the Millennium Force at the Amusement Park. I shake that thought from my mind because I knew there was no way I was right in my thinking. Levi his hot headed and Jax is crazy... I shake my head trying to release those thought because it just couldn't be possible.

"I don't know man, you know Jax is going to have his head after that beat down." One guy says gesturing his hand as if he were shooting a gun.

I felt sick. That's all I needed to definitely confirm the truth. *Why Levi? Why?* I kept repeating in my head.

"Alright class lets settle down," the teacher says. "I know it's hard to after all that commotion but we must get to work or else you guys can do the lesson at home and turn it in for homework."

Everyone who weren't seated scrambled to their seat in a hurry and acted like they were eager to learn and get started with the lesson. I however, couldn't concentrate. If I had my phone I'd double text or even triple text Levi until he answered. I would even text, Gia to see if she knew anything but I couldn't even do that. I felt completely lost and out of the loop without my cell.

I raise my hand to get the teacher's attention. "I need to use the restroom." She glances at me from above the rim of her glasses and stares as if I was disrupting her teaching time. She ignores me and turns back around to continue writing on the board. "I really need to go! I feel sick." This time she didn't even turn around. She acted as if I were lying and used this excuse to get out of class all the time.

Everyone started snickering and cracking some kind of jokes about how the teacher played me. I exhale loudly and finally my hand comes down out of the air and smacks the desk making a loud sound.

Normally I'd just deal with it but teachers like this really piss me off. I'd never given this lady any back talk or anything the way these other kids do. There was really no reason for her to treat me this way.

I close my text book and pack it away sitting on the edge of my seat wondering if I should make a run for it. I wait for a few more minutes trying to give this lady respect to just not walk out of her class but she's making it hard.

I throw my book bag onto my shoulders and high tail it out of class and head to the main office. That's where Levi would be it were him that were fighting.

CHAPTER 13
LEVI

◦⌒◦

I'm sitting in the office with a bag of ice on my hand and a cop standing in between Jax and I. That was just a tactic to make sure Jax and I don't go after each other again.

The school didn't call the cops. They're here every day because they patrol the school. They're not security guards either. Every day we enter the building we have to go through metal detectors and every so often we have random searches after going through the detectors. We have to stand in line and watch them go through our bags.

When I was a freshman and had to go through that the first time, I was pissed. Not because I had something to hide, I just felt violated like it was an invasion of my privacy or something.

It not like our school was that bad. But then again, maybe it wasn't that bad because of these tactics. That's how I knew Jax wouldn't have a weapon on him.

He told the principal that I came at him first. *Guilty as charged.* I did come after him, and I'd do it again in a heartbeat over, Nyla, but I didn't tell the principal that. I haven't said not one word. They're saying I'm being uncooperative just because I won't talk. It's nobody's business why I did what I did. I know why I did it and that's all that matters.

I glance over at, Jax and he keeps staring at me smiling. *Smile all you want asshole, you won't be seeing out that left eye by tomorrow.* But most importantly, he won't be at school tomorrow and that way, Nyla can have a few days of not having to worry about seeing his ass.

Anyway of course they called my parents. I knew mom couldn't come so dad has to leave work. I'm waiting on him to get here now. I keep telling these dumb asses that I drive to school and I can just go home but they want to speak to an adult. *Whatever man.*

I see, Nyla through the glass window coming this way. My stomach drops. I'm not sure if she'll feel honored I fought for her or if she'll be pissed. With my luck she'll be pissed.

She walks into the office and then freezes when she sees Jax.

"I know damn well you betta be coming to see me," Jax says to Nyla.

Her eyes go from me to Jax and back again. I

can tell he has her scared out of her mind so I don't say anything. I can just talk to her later. *Somehow.* I'm not going to make her make that kind of choice when I know she wants to choose me, anyway.

She slowly backs out of the office and we keep eye contact the whole time until she's gone. I knew she was coming to check on me. That's all that matters.

Twenty minutes later my dad and I are seated in the principal's office and he fills my dad in on what took place.

"Okay. So how long is he going to be out?" My dad asks, and the principal looks at him as if he wanted my father to go off on me or something.

"Sir, I don't think you understand the magnitude of this altercation," the principal said.

"With all due respect, I think I understand a little more than you do."

The principal sighed and ignored my father's comment. "We have a zero tolerance for fighting in this school. Technically that's grounds for expulsion."

"Expulsion?" My dad questions. "My son hasn't been suspended before. Isn't there a certain number of days that equals the first, second, and third offense?"

"Normally, yes... but..."

There was a commotion going on outside the principal's office and my dad and I were the first ones out of the door because it sounds like, Gigi's voice.

"You put your hands on my brother!" Gigi's hanging over, Jax beating him on the head.

"Get off me, bitch!" Jax pushes my sister so hard she falls to the floor. That's all my dad, and I needed to see. My dad goes to help, Gia up to make sure she's alright while I make my way over to, Jax to beat his ass again.

The secretary doesn't yell or say anything. She just moves out of the way and calls, "Security!" over the loud speaker.

Within seconds the cops are all over Jax and I. My father was trying to break us up and I could hear him yelling but I just couldn't bring myself to stop.

I try my best to fight my dad off of me but it wasn't him trying to get ahold of me. "Stop resisting!" The cop shouts.

"Lee, stop!" I can now hear my sister and dad yell to me.

"I will taser you!" Another cop stood in front of me holding something that resembled a gun. I stop and try to hold my hands up but it was too late. The other cop was already slamming me onto the hard floor that definitely felt like cold concrete and jams his knee into the middle of my back.

"Hold on, now! Hold on! I'll get him!" I hear my dad shout over Gia's cries.

"Step back, sir!" The cop with the taser warns my dad.

I feel pain and numb at the same time. The way the cop is pressing his knee into my back feels like he's breaking my ribs in two. By instinct my hands try to go to where the pain on my body hurts the most but he shouts again and mushes my head more onto the floor. "I said stop resisting!"

"I'm. not. resisting." I manage to get out. "Hurt,"

I groan in pain. He finally has my hands handcuffed behind me and two cops help me to my feet.

The main office is in the front of the building surrounded by a wall of glass so it wasn't hard for me to hear and see more cop cars when they pull up with sirens blazing.

The cop who handcuffed me is reading me my Maranda Rights. "Why am I being arrested?" The cop ignores me and raises his voice an octave to continue. I look at me dad, "Dad?" I yell to him.

"This is a bit extreme, don't you think?" My dad says to anyone who would listen but nobody was.

"We got him." Two black officers say as they walk Jax outside and put him into the back of their police car.

"Why doesn't he have to be handcuffed?" Gia asks.

"That's his father," the principal answers.

"Well why the hell can't I take my son?"

"Your son's the assailant," the cop said. "And he was resisting after he was warned many times."

"My son is hurt and needs medical attention," my dad says.

"It's not life threatening. He'll get medical attention after he's booked."

"I would like to take a picture of my son's injuries before you take him to make sure nothing else happens to him."

"Nothing will happen to him as long as he complies," the officer says sternly.

As they were walking me towards the exit, I hear the principal call to my dad and sister to talk about her suspension for putting her hands on another student, meaning Jax.

"Yeah, yeah," My dad groans. "I'm taking her with me right now. We'll find out how longs she's out for when you send the papers to the house. Right now, I need to follow my son and make sure he's okay."

CHAPTER 14
NYLA

I looked for Gia everywhere at school and couldn't find her. People said she and Levi got arrested but I know that couldn't be true. But now I'm wondering because neither of them were anywhere to be found. This would be a lot easier if I just had my phone.

"Mom," I call out to her. She was in the kitchen cooking dinner. I walk up and throw my arms around her waist hugging her from behind.

"What do you want, Nyla?" She questions me.

I release her and ask, "Do you need any help?"

"Yes, you can finish seasoning the rest of the chicken."

I wash my hands and begin to season the

chicken. My stomach was doing all types of backflips trying to muster up enough courage to ask for my phone back.

"I'm sorry for not being honest about my feelings for, Levi," I say.

She exhales and removes the cooked chicken from the oil and places it into the strainer. She glances at me, "You know, I wouldn't have let you stay over there if I knew you and that boy had feelings for one another."

"I know, mom." She flours more chicken and lays it into the hot oil piece by piece sending the oil into a sizzling frenzy. "We weren't even that serious about each other at that time."

"Serious? So, you guys are serious?" She stops flouring chicken and looks at me. "Are you saying that sending you over there was my fault?"

I close my eyes mentally counting to ten. She has been so hard to talk to and deal with lately, it's annoying. "That's not what I'm saying mom."

"I just don't understand what has gotten into you, Nyla. Are you having a hard time adjusting to the fact that Daniel and I got married? Or that you have and instant sister? Or that I'm pregnant?"

It may have been all of those things, but I'm adjusting to it. All of it. *I just need my phone back.* "Mom, can I please have my phone back?" If I didn't hurry and ask now, it may have never come out of my mouth.

She stops stirring the mac n' cheese and tosses the spoon onto the countertop. Noodles and cheese splashes and land over the counter. "So that's what this little mother-daughter time is? Just a ploy to ask for that damn phone?"

I jump and frown because it wasn't like that at all. I hugged her to soften her up a bit but also because I can't remember the last time we hugged. It was nice being in the kitchen cooking again just the two of us and talking. Even though the conversation wasn't going as well as I thought it would. I guess life was just simpler when the topic didn't revolve around boys.

"No, mom. But I really need my phone back." I try to plead with her. "I really need to check on, Levi and Gia. There was this huge fight today at school and I heard they both got arrested."

It was like horror took over her face. "Why would they get arrested? And Gia at that?"

"I don't know. That's what I'm trying to find out."

"Now I know I made the right decision," she says putting her hands on her hips.

"Please mom, I'll give the phone back as soon as I'm done."

She looks like she's seriously thinking about my request until a knock on the door interrupts her thoughts. "See who's at the door."

Stupid freaking door! Who cares who's at the door! I'm trying to find out about my boyfriend and best friend. Ugh! I march to the door asking, "Who is it?" And yank it open without waiting for a reply.

My stomach falls to my feet and stays there and so does my mouth. I couldn't believe my eyes. "Dad!"

CHAPTER 15
LEVI

W e're sitting in the police station and they've finally uncuffed me because I'm not posing a threat to them, I guess. But something is just not sitting right with me. Jax's father is a cop. That's crazy. I would have never imaged that ever. Does his father know how he is? That he carries a gun and terrorizes people? Does he even know that he's raped someone?

As I look over at Jax and his father, I'm guessing they have a cool relationship because they're laughing and joking like this isn't serious business. By looking at them you would think it's bring your son to work day.

The other cop comes back to his desk and sits with us. "Okay," He exhales loudly. "They're not going to press charges." *He's saying this as if we should be thankful.* Like all this was my fault, and I had no justifiable reason to beat his ass.

I want to tell him about what, Jax did to, Nyla but something inside me tells me to shut up because *one*, either they're not going to believe me, or *two*, they're on his side from the get-go and it would just be a cover up.

"Thank you, sir. Where do we go from here?" My dad asks like he's grateful and there is no underlying problem here.

"Well, all charges are dropped so you're free to go. A bit of advice?" He leans in closer to me as if he were my friend about to share his deepest darkest secret with me. "Don't do that again," he warned then leans back up and his mood changes. "Fighting is never the answer. Someone could have gotten seriously hurt today."

My dad must have taken some kind of offense to what was said. "My son has never been into any type of trouble before. Never even gotten suspended." He glances over at, Jax. "Truth be told, we've had problems with this fella here before." He points in, Jax's direction nonchalantly with is thumb over his shoulders.

"Is that right?" The cop leans in a little more edging my father on for more info.

"As a matter of fact, they've gotten into it before." He was referring to, Jax and I. "This boy has come to my house and threatened my son and our whole family." My father leans in a little closer and lowers his voice. "This animosity is going on because that boy, raped a young girl we know."

The officer sits back with a worried look on his face. "Raped? Well why hasn't anyone filed a report on that?"

"I believe the child's mother has." He glances in my direction. "Isn't that right, son?"

"Yea," I nod my head in agreement.

After the officer types some things into a computer he says while shaking his head, "Nope. I don't see anything in here. There were no charges filed against, Jaxson. Especially not rape."

My dad and I both sit back with knots on our foreheads trying to figure out why there were no charges filed. I know for a fact, Nyla said the police came out and they filed a report. But I haven't heard anything else about it since then.

"That's odd," my dad says.

"Very odd," I agree.

***

When we pull up to the house, it was dawn. We could see the sun going down. It looked huge with an orange glow to it. It was peaceful. The three of us sit in the car gazing at it as if it was taking our stress and this long hard day along with it.

I glance over at our front door and mom has the door open, probably with the screen door locked. Aside from her fear of being outdoors she's scared as hell of being at home alone especially when it gets dark. She says if something's in the house she wants to be sure she can get out fast. Dad and I both try to tell her she's safer inside with the door locked because these days anybody can come in and get her. She says it's not people she's worried about. That part, I never understood.

"Not a word to mom about, Lee being arrested," my dad says. "I'm not telling you guys to lie."

"We get it daddy," Gia says.

My dad wanted to drop, Gigi off at home first because he knew mom would be worried and scared. But he was more scared of me being arrested and in the hands of the cops. Nowadays, it's the cops you fear the most. Too many people have lost their lives innocently and mysteriously at the hands of cops. I'd never seen my dad fear anything the way he was shaking and nervous today. I'm not going to bring that up to him unless he does first and want to talk about it. Fear and being scared is nothing to be ashamed about, but it can be a blow to a man's ego and I'm not going to do that to my father.

We walk into the house and mom's curled up on the couch hugging her knees watching cartoons. That's what she does when she's afraid. She said she's done that since she was a young girl, but she would never watch, Scooby Doo because even their monsters scared her even if it were just a mask in the end.

"Where have you guys been?" Mom says as she jumps to her feet. "What happened to you?" She runs to me examining my face. It's not that it's as bad as, Jax but I'm sure anyone could tell that I'd been fighting. He got some good licks in.

"He got into a fight at school," My dad says.

"I know that, Eli!" Mom shoots dad an evil look. "Why the hell does anyone have phones if no one's going to answer them?"

"My battery went out," dad says. "You know how crazy my battery's been acting lately."

"I lost my phone in the fight, ma. I'm sure it's crushed to death," I say.

She looks over at, Gigi expecting an answer and I couldn't even think of one for her. We both look at dad for a way out.

"They're both suspended. When I was in the office with, Lee... Gigi was out there getting her pounds in on the guy too." Dad says trying to deflect the last question.

"You were fighting a dude?" Mom shrieks and then runs over to Gigi to examines her. "Did he hurt you? Not every guy is your brother, Gigi!"

We went through the whole story about Gigi fighting Jax and then how I jump in and fight him again, omitting the part about the cops of course.

"Okay, so again what took so damn long?" We stayed silent and look to dad for answers and he was looking at us with the same expression. "So, nobody's going to tell me the part about the cops and how they arrested, Lee?" Mom says with her arms folded across her chest peering straight into dad's eyes.

"How the hell did you find out about that?" Dad says.

"How the hell did you think I wouldn't?"

Dad rubs the back of his neck and exhales. "Nini, I was trying to save you some anguish of not having to deal with that." Dad tried to appeal to mom's softer side by using her nickname. I always chuckle a bit to myself when I hear it because it's so close to her real name. Same syllables and same spelling just changing the 'a' to 'i' at the end.

"You think getting arrested is funny, Lee? You think it's a joke?" Mom goes in on me.

"What? No!" "I'm sitting up here thinking about this woman and smiling to myself and she's taking things the wrong way.

"OMG, Lee! Look at this... your video is going viral!" Gigi shoves her cell in my face.

"What video?" The four of us are looking at this video of me that someone recorded when the cop had slammed me onto the floor and pressed his knee into my back. I look at, Gia and shake my head. She could have waited until we weren't around mom or dad if she wanted to show me this.

My mom jumps. "Oh. My. Gosh!" She snatches the phone from my hands and watches it about a million more times. "Do you see this, Eli?"

"Yes, Nina... I was there," my dad grunts.

"Why were you resisting, Lee?" My mom questions me.

"Ma, it wasn't as bad as it looks. I wasn't resisting I was trying to grab my rib because it was hurting and he was pressing me on that hard floor."

My mom had tears in her eyes and was on the verge of crying. She closed her eyes and raised her right hand as she shook her head. "Thank you, Jesus for your angels of protection!"

"Yes, yes, yes," My dad says in agreement.

We all stand there for a moment in silence.

I lay in my bed thinking about, Nyla and for a brief moment I'm wondering why she hasn't called. It just dawned on me that neither one of us has phones.

CHAPTER 16
NYLA

Packing.
I'm freaking packing!
I can't believe this.

I have no idea what I'm doing because I'm crying so hard I can't see. All this time I said I wanted to go live with my dad and mom said no. Now all of a sudden when, Levi and I are the closest we have to be light-years apart.

I feel like my mom is doing whatever she can in her power to just ruin my life. *I don't have a say in anything!* Why is it called, *'my life'* when clearly, it's *her* life? Why couldn't I just wait and go this summer? *But nooooo!* They want to uproot me now! Why???

I'm throwing clothes into my suitcase and duffle bag. I have no idea what I'm even taking and right now I don't care.

"Here, let me help you," Camila says touching my things on my bed.

I snatch them out of her hands. "Move!" I yell at her. I don't care if I hurt her feelings or not. Nobody cares about mine. "You just can't wait until I'm out of here, huh?"

She backs up and fold her arms across her chest. Her face crinkles and then returns to normal like she was going to say something but changed her mind. "Believe it or not, I'm just as pissed as you. I don't understand why your mom is doing this? And why like this and so soon?"

I stare at her like I'm searching for the answers to the same questions. I can't help it but looking at, Camila right now has me only thinking about one thing. Levi.

What happens when I leave? Will they become closer in some attempt of so-called missing me? Was her friendship just a ploy waiting for this exact moment so she could pounce on him? Did she know my mom was planning to send me to my dad's? She always seemed to know everything else before I did.

My heart jolts and I look at my closed bedroom door and then back at, Camila. "Can I use your phone, please?" I beg as if I were begging for my life.

She acted as if she really had to think about it. "Okay. I know you need to talk to your man," she teased.

I try to remember, Levi's number by heart because I wasn't used to dialing it. I usually just push a button. I roll my eyes because I knew I had the right number after I dialed it and *<hearteyes emoji> Cutie <hearteyes emoji>* came up as the phone was connecting. I frown and turn the phone around to show, Camila I did not approve.

"Oh, my bad. I meant to change that," she grimaces.

"Ugh!" His phone went straight to voicemail. I hope he wasn't ignoring the call because he saw, Camila's number pop up. But then that thought made me smile if he did. "He's not answering," I say aloud, not necessarily to, Camila.

I give up on, Levi and bite the bullet and dial, Gia. Now, I didn't mind talking to her. I wanted to hear her voice. I needed to hear her voice. I needed her to tell me we're cool and everything will be okay.

The phone rings twice and I jump pressing the end button on, Camila's phone when my mom burst through the door. "You just about ready?"

Before I say anything, I slide, Camila's phone into her hand without my mom seeing. "Just can't wait to get rid of me, huh?" I turn back around and shove random things into a bag.

"Camila, can you give us a minute?" My mom walks completely into the room and stands next to me.

"Sure, why not," Camila says pulling herself from her bed and closing the door behind her.

"I thought this is what you wanted," she said sticking her bottom lip out like she was pouting.

"Since when do you care about giving me what

I wanted?" I don't care about being disrespectful. I wanted to say so much more using words I'm not allowed to use yet, or to her *ever*.

"Look, Nyla. When I discussed this with your father, it was in the heat of the moment. I let my emotions get the better of me."

I don't care about your excuses or your damn pregnancy brain! That's what my mind said, not me. "I appreciate you keeping me in the loop of what I'm doing with my life, mom."

"Nyla, I thought I had time to talk to you about this. I thought he would give me enough time to even change my mind." She kept looking at me as if I were going to respond to that. I didn't. I just kept on packing. "He wasn't even supposed to be here until two weeks from now."

"So, go out there and tell him, I'm not going. That you changed your mind."

My mom leans against my bed, "I can't do that. He took a flight all the way here, Nyla."

"So!" They were both getting on my nerves right about now. They both were acting like I don't have a say-so on what I want. "Can I at least have my cell back?" *That's the least you could do.*

"No. I stand firm on that, Nyla."

"Why not?" I whine. "I'm going to be so many miles away from, Gia and Levi. You really want me to have no contact at all?"

"Yes, Nyla. I mean that. I told your father about your punishment too. He promises to honor my wishes. If I give you that phone back, I'm defeating the purpose of sending you to your father's.

"You're unreal, mom! I hate you!" I meant that with everything I had in me. How and why was she being so cruel to me? I snatch up my bags and take them out the front door.

I didn't want to hug her. Say goodbye to her or anyone in that house. Ever since she married, Daniel my life has gone downhill all because my mother changed.

CHAPTER 17
LEVI

∾

It was almost seven o'clock in the morning but it looked like it was night. A dark grayish hue covered everything as far as I could see. I don't know if it was because I was sleepy as hell but everything seemed to be black and white as if I were colorblind. The rain poured at a steady rate as thunder rumbled in the distance.

I backed into a secluded parking space so I could see, Nyla when her mom dropped her off but she wouldn't be able to see me. Of course, if she looked hard enough she could. Another reason I was hiding because I didn't want anyone to see me because I wasn't supposed to be on school property.

I turn the ignition back on and blast the air conditioner. Not because I was hot but because I kept nodding off and I needed something to keep my eyes open. I use my sweatshirt to wipe the windshield so I could see out clearly.

Finally, I spot, Nyla's mom's car pull up to the drop-off spot and I wait for, Nyla to get out. The hardest part? Getting, Nyla's attention before she goes into the building but after her mom pulls off.

An umbrella shoots out from the passenger side and she scurries inside the building with the rest of the people trying to run from the rain. *Damn!* It's not like I can just go into the building and catch her at her locker. Security would know it's me as soon as I step in.

Wait.

Why is her mom going into the building too? I throw my hands into the air and give up. I can't even use Gigi's phone to call, Camila because I don't know her number by heart. *Dammit!*

Wait.

Where the hell is, Camila anyway?

Forget it.

I give up and head back home to come up with a better plan. By the time I reach home, I'm asking myself why I am trying so hard to get in touch with her when we should be trying to get in touch with me as well.

"What are you doing up so early?" My mom asks as I walk in.

"I went to the gas station to get some gas and a Polar pop." I hold the carrier up in my hand. "And I bought you and dad coffee too."

"Thanks, now I don't have to make any because dad is running late for work, anyway."

Mom grabs both coffees and hand one to dad as she kisses him out the door. She sits on the couch next to me. "You want to talk about it?"

"Noooo, mom." I had no idea what she was talking about. I didn't know if she wanted to talk to me about what happened yesterday or, Nyla. I didn't want to discuss either one.

"Oh my gosh!"

Mom and I sit up on the couch as we hear, Gigi scream. She comes running down the stairs. "What's the matter?"

Gia's standing there staring at her phone like she just found out that somebody died. "Gia what is it?" I was about to get up and shake the words out of her.

"That, Camila girl just text me," she says looking up from her phone. "Nyla's gone!"

CHAPTER 18
NYLA

‿○

Who takes a plane in the middle of the night? I feel like I was placed into a witness protection program and no one knows where I am.

A three-and-a-half-hour flight. I slept the whole time because it was way past my bedtime, anyway. You would think dad and I would have this big massive get-to-know me again conversation, but we didn't. Even if he wanted to talk, I wouldn't have. *I hope, Camila got in touch with Gia and Levi to let them know what happened.*

I stand in the doorway of my dad's apartment and stare. This place was immaculate, and I didn't even see the whole place yet.

"You want a quick tour before I bring up the rest of your bags?" I shake my head no. I still don't feel like talking. "I know you have a lot to sort out in your mind, so I'll give you some space to do so. Let me show you to your room."

My room was not my room. It was a guest room, and that's exactly what I felt like... a guest. It was nice though, it just wasn't mine. Everything in this room was neutral. Just grey. I like color. Pink to be exact.

My duffle bag fell from my shoulder and onto the floor. That's exactly where I left it. I sat on the bed expecting to sink it, but no. It was as hard as a brick. I lift the corner of the sheet just to make sure it wasn't sheetrock.

I fall back onto the bed and now I think I have a concussion.

Wow. This is next level punishment. I have no communication devices at all. I might as well be in a posh prison. *Way to go mom.*

I must have drifted off for about an hour. At least that's what the clock on the nightstand says. It's not like I can check the time on my cell.

"I made some food. Why don't you come and eat with me?" My dad says standing in the doorway.

Sure, why not. It didn't sound like I had much choice, anyway. Besides, I was starving.

When I get to the table my stomach immediately growls and my mouth waters. The food looked so yummy. It was pancakes, bacon, and eggs. Except the eggs looked a bit suspect. They were white. Too white. All white.

I frown a little when I don't see my Mrs.

Butterworth's syrup. Like seriously, that's the only syrup I eat! *Fine.* I won't be a brat, I'll eat whatever this generic Alaga syrup is. You would think with all the money dad has he'd be able to afford better syrup.

I pour gobs of the stuff over my pancakes because I love a lot of syrup. I position the cut into my pancakes just right so there's a pool of syrup in the middle and it won't touch my bacon or eggs. I stuff my mouth with pancakes and instantly I want to vomit! I have no idea what's going on in my mouth right now.

"Everything okay?" My dad asks.

I don't know if I should tell him the truth, spit this crap out of my mouth, or run to the bathroom to throw it all up. I swallow it down instead and vow to never eat another bite of that crap.

WTF! Why is the bacon like rubber and the eggs like water? I can't take it anymore! "What am I eating?" I say with disgust not being able to hold it in any longer.

"What do you mean?" My dad looks at me as if I asked him a trick question.

"Seriously dad, what is this crap?"

"You don't like my cooking?" He frowns.

"Actually, I don't think it's your cooking skills that's the problem. It might be the ingredients and condiments."

He laughs, "you don't like the syrup or the pancakes?"

I don't like any of it! But I can't say that because it would be too insensitive and ungrateful. "What brand of stuff do you use?" *Maybe that's the problem.*

"It's wheat pancakes, egg whites, and turkey bacon."

That's it! I can't stay here. There's no way I'm going to be able to do it! I push my plate away and cover my hands with my mouth. "What are you on a diet or something?"

"What?" He glances up at me confused as he was about to finish up his plate. "It's heart healthy. It's good for you, honey."

"Do you have a heart condition I don't know about? Did your doctor prescribe this stuff or something?"

"No," he says chuckling again. "That could be why I don't. I'm all about preventive care. Why wait to change your eating habits after the fact."

I guess that made sense, but still. "Dad! That's all good for you, but I'm sixteen! I love sweets and junk food." I pick up his syrup and point it at him. "And syrup that taste good! You must know how bad it tastes because you didn't even eat any."

"I don't eat syrup, honey. I got that for you." *Why have pancakes if you're not going to use syrup?* I give up and lay my head on the table. "Let me make you something else to eat."

"Forget it, dad. I don't think you have anything in here that's edible for me," I say without lifting my head. "I'm just going to wither away and starve to death."

After a few moments my head pops up. "Dad, where's your home phone?"

"I don't have one."

"Why not?" I get angry all over again.

"Because I use my cellular phone. Having a home phone for me is just another useless bill."

"Well, can I use your phone?" I whine.

"Sure. I guess you should call your mom and let her know we made it safely. I know how close you two are." *Ha. Not anymore.*

I go to my *guest room* and immediately dial Gia's number after, Levi's went to voicemail again. I call her three times in a row before she answers.

"Hello?" She sounds annoyed.

"Gia!" I whisper and don't know why I do.

"OMG! Nyla?" I hear shuffling over the phone. "Guys! It's Nyla on the phone!" She yells. "What's going on? Where the heck are you?"

Instant tears stream down my face. "I-I'm in Cali at my dad's."

"Are you serious! Camila texted me but I wasn't sure if I should believe her or not."

"Yea, it's true."

"Lee, has been freaking out. Why didn't you tell us?"

Levi. He probably was thinking the worse. "Where is he? How is he? Did you guys really get arrested?"

"Right here. He's fine. And yea he did, but they dropped the charges."

Before Gia or I could get anything else out, Levi grabs the phone. "Babe? Where are you? Please don't say Cali." His voice breaks.

"I-I am."

"You left me?" I hear a door slam in the background.

"I didn't have a choice." I choke back my tears. "I didn't even know, Levi.

"You're gone? For real? Just like that?"

"Mhm." I couldn't speak words.

42

"Okay, but for how long? When will you be back? I mean you have school and everything."

"I dunno. They're putting me in an online school."

"So, what about us?" I'm silent because I'm just trying to soak, Levi's voice in. My heart is hurting so bad and I want to be with him right now. *I feel sick.* "Nyla," he calls my name and my heart breaks into a million pieces.

"I love you, Levi."

I'm waiting for him to say it back. To tell me he loves me too and no matter what we'll make it work. But he doesn't. Instead the line goes dead. My heart jumps and I'm thinking we lost connection so I call back. This time twice before, Gia answers again.

"Hey, Nyla..." She says dryly.

"Where's Levi? We got disconnected."

"I know. He hung up."

I shatter and fall to pieces. "What do you mean he hung up? Why?"

"He's hurt, Nyla," she sighs. "It's kind of ironic. Honestly, I didn't want you guys to be together because I didn't want him to hurt you. But now it's my brother who's hurt... and you did it."

What the hell just happened? How did we all go from excitement to doom and gloom? "What the hell, Gia? You're acting like I wanted to leave. Like I wanted to hurt *your* brother. It's not my fault! I'm hurting too!"

"Now you know how I felt. You think I wanted you to get raped? You don't think it hurt me that you were hurting? You shut me out, Nyla. For no good reason and I was supposed to be your best

43

friend."

"Really, Gia?"

"I need to go check on my brother."

I sat there stunned. Confused. Hurt. This cannot be happening to me right now. I gave my dad back his phone and lay down on this sheetrock and cried until I fell asleep.

CHAPTER 19
LEVI

I can't believe it.

I can't believe she up and left me like that. I don't know why but I feel like such a fool. How could she not know she was leaving town? I get it now. Her urgency to get a room and then the next day saying we should keep our distance. Blaming it all on the fear of, Jax.

Played.

That's what she did to me. Man, this shit hurts like hell. I wish she would have just left me the hell alone.

"Hey, big brother." Gigi pokes her head in the door.

"Not right now, Gia. Please." I sniff and wipe my face with my hands. I don't want my sister to see me crying over her best friend who she warned me not to be with.

"Aww c'mere." She sits next to me and put her arms around me.

"Gone, Gigi." I shove her off.

"Lee, talk to me."

"Why?"

"Because you need somebody to talk to, Lee and right now all you have is mommy and me. Until daddy gets off work if you'd prefer to talk to him."

"I don't want to talk to nobody, damn!"

"Calm down, Lee, acting like a butt hurt whipped puppy." She rolls her eyes. "Just be glad y'all wasn't in a serious relationship and then slept together... now that would be some hurt fo yo ass." She nudged me trying to make light of the situation and make me feel better. Instead I felt worse.

I look at my sister, "can you just leave." I blink and tears run down my face. I try to catch them as fast as I could but it was too late.

"Oh, hecks no!" Gigi gets up and hops around my floor like she has to pee. "Lee. No. wheeeeennn?"

I don't even care no more. "A couple days ago," I sniff.

"Are you freakin' kidding me!" She sits next to me like she was thinking of something to say. "Okay, well at least she wasn't your first. I think that would hurt worse for a longer amount of time and be harder to get over."

I shake my head and look at my sister with

squinted eyes. "She was my first, Gigi." The look on my sister's face was shock. Why the hell was this such a shock to everybody? "Gia, please get out... you're not helping."

"I'm so sorry, bro." I know she was but there wasn't nothing she or anybody could do about the way I was feeling.

I missed dinner. I just didn't feel like eating. I didn't have an appetite, not for food anyway. I know they'll put my plate up for when I get ready. I thank them for that and leaving me the hell alone for a few hours.

"LEE! GETUP!" My mom stands in front of me putting two separate words together.

I don't flinch because her yelling doesn't scare me. "Mom, whaaaat?"

"Sit up!" She says yanking the covers from me. I still don't move. "You and Nyla had sex?"

I jump up. "Who told you that?" I glare at, Gigi in the doorway.

"Dang, Ma... way to keep a secret."

"You're telling me, Gia!" I shake my head. "I'm not telling you shit again."

My mom pops me in my lips a few times. I throw up my arms to block her from doing it again. It wasn't hard, more like a bum-bump. "Watch your mouth, Lee! So, it is true."

I don't talk, I just stare at, Gia with my arms folded.

"Good-bye, RaGia Marie Nash!" Gia knew that whenever mom says your full government, she meant business. Gigi bolted from my room. *That's what she gets.*

"Now you! Who the hell told you, you were allowed to have sex?" *Is she serious? What kind of question was that?*

"Nobody said I was allowed. That's why we didn't have sex here."

"Well, thaaaank youuuu for at least following one rule!" She stares at me for a moment like she wanted me to say, you're welcome. "Did you at least cover up?"

"What?" I'm seriously laughing inside because mom is so mad and I don't understand why? I'm about to be eighteen soon. Surely, I deserve a good job for that.

"You know. Did you use something?" She said talking with her hands.

She was so uncomfortable talking about this with me and I don't know why she didn't just have dad come in. Knowing mom, she was too impatient to wait on dad. He kinda takes a while, like days. But I couldn't resist playing with her. She kinda reminded me of, Nyla. They'd rather dance around certain words instead of coming right out and saying it. Like now, I knew mom was referring to me wearing a condom with, Nyla but I'm not letting her off the hook that easily.

"Something like what?" I cringe like I didn't know what she was talking about.

"Are you kidding me! This goes to show that you're not mature enough to have sex if you don't know I'm talking about a prophylactic." *Did she really just say prophylactic!* I'm dying inside.

"And maybe you shouldn't even have two kids right now if you can't say condom, mom, but then again maybe that's why you do." My mom took a step back with her jaw dropped like I literally said a cuss word. "C'mon mom, why don't you go have this conversation with, Gigi and leave the man stuff to dad."

"It's not funny, Lee." My mom throws her soft punches to my shoulder because I can't stop laughing.

Dad comes in and puts his arms around mom and kisses her forehead gently. Sometimes it was gross when my parents display their PDA in front of us. But not now. For some reason, now I get it and it's not so gross anymore. It just makes me miss, Nyla more even though I'm mad as hell at her right now.

"It's okay, babe. You did good." Dad said to mom.

"He's a damn fool, he's not listening to me, Eli." Mom says cutting her eyes at me.

"I know," Dad says chuckling a bit. I knew he wanted to laugh just like I did. "I'll take it from here."

I'm so glad dad is here. Dealing with mom about this issue was just too awkward. Plus believe it or not, dad can be a little more lenient than mom. When we were younger, mom used to tear me and Gigi's butt up when we got in trouble. But as I got older, her hits just weren't doing much for me. It was so bad I couldn't even fake cry. So, then it went to, *"Just wait until your father gets home."* Nine times out of ten, dad would be tired as hell coming in from work and mom would expected him to go straight to my room and whoop my butt, it didn't even matter if I was sleeping. A few times he'd come in and shut the door and whack the belt a few times on something that sounded like my ass and instruct me to cry out and I did. Yup. That was dad's and I little secret. I never even told, Gigi. Dad said I was too big to be getting a whooping but if I did something really bad, then me and him was going to have to take it outside and knuckle up man to man. Thank God it never came to that.

"What's going on, son?" Dad pulls a folding chair out and sits on it so that we're face to face.

"Nothing," I say as I stretch and then scratch my head. "Everything, seems like lately." I exhale.

"I get it," dad says nodding his head. "You and Nyla are pretty serious, I hear."

"Yea."

"Okay. Nothing wrong with that." *I take it back. This conversation is awkward no matter which parent it is.* "Do *you* have any questions?" *Uh, no. If I did I think it would be a little too late for that.*

"I don't have any questions about sex, dad."

"Okay, what do you have questions about?"

"I'm pissed, dad! I'm angry. And I can't do anything about it."

"You're pissed, huh?" I nod my head. *Duh.* "Usually when you're angry, Lee... You hit something. I've got split wood and patched holes in the walls to prove it." *Ohhh kay...* "Maybe you are angry, Lee but maybe you're more depressed."

"Depressed? I am not depressed, dad."

"Lee, there's a thin line between anger and depression. I think you may have crossed over the angry line and slid head first into depression. Now I'm not saying you need a doctor or pills. I'm just calling it like I see it." I shake my head in disagreement. "You're not eating, you've been sleeping all day. Son, I'm not a doctor but I'd say you have a clear case of heartbreak."

"You said all that just to say, Nyla broke my heart?"

"If that's all you got out of it, then yes."

"Really, dad? I could have told you that. What I want to know is how to get rid of it."

He sits and thinks for a moment. "I don't think you can get rid of it. It's more or less that you have to learn to deal with it and adjust until it just doesn't hurt so much."

I slam my head into my hands because I feel like nobody was telling me what I needed to do to make my heart not hurt so bad.

"I'll tell you what. I'd rather for you to be angry. That way you can punch something or get up off your ass and do something about your situation." He places his hand on my knee. "I give you permission to knock as many holes in the wall that you need to. Just don't hit anybody. And don't hurt yourself. I can patch the walls better than I can patch you up." He sits back and chuckles. "But your mother did ask a serious question that you still haven't answered."

Oh my gosh, why??? "Is this the condom question again?" He nods. "No dad. I didn't strap up."

Disappointment forms in his face. "Why son? I know we've had this conversation before."

Because it was, Nyla! My first love. My first girl. My first everything and I didn't want anything in between us, not even a thin piece of pigskin. I say nothing. I just sat there not knowing what to say to him.

"Lee, it's not just called protection for nothing. It protects you from diseases and unwanted babies." *Maybe I wouldn't mind getting, Nyla pregnant. Maybe.*

"Dad, I don't need the PSA, I learned that much in health class."

"Okay, okay... I'm not going to preach."

I glance around at the walls as soon as my dad left out. For some reason having permission to be angry and let out my frustrations freely without repercussions had an opposite effect on me. Now that it was okay to punch a hole in the wall I had no desire to do so. *Maybe that's what they mean by reverse psychology.*

CHAPTER 20
NYLA

"**M**om," I cry into the phone. "Why do you hate me so much?"

"I don't hate you, Nyla. Everything I do, every choice I make on your behalf is to protect you. You might not understand that now, but when you have a child, you will understand."

"But I was going to have my own child, and you stopped it."

"Everything happens for a reason. Even if you don't understand it now. That boy used you, Nyla. He didn't care about you. You would have been living that same life as the girl he already had pregnant or worse."

"But I love, Levi and he loves me mom."

"I don't doubt that the two of you think you're in

love."

"I want to come home, mom. I miss you. Please don't punish me anymore. Dad is nice, but he's not you. I miss the way we were."

"Nyla... Nyla."

I wake up and the room is pitch black. How long had I been sleeping?

"Did you talk to your mother?"

"Yea," I say trying to focus on my surrounding.

"She said you would lie about it." My dad says flicking on the light and now I'm blind.

"Lie about what?" I rub my neck because the sheetrock has me feeling stiff.

"You told me earlier that you were calling your mother to let her know we arrived safely. Instead I'm guessing you called this boy she forbids you to have communication with."

"Oh, I must have dreamt that I talked to her."

"What's going on with you? At first, I was taking the things your crazy mother was saying with a grain of salt, but now I'm not so sure."

"Dad, I'm not lying. I was dreaming I was talking to mom when I said I spoke with her."

He shakes his head and tsk. "We'll discuss this at a later date. I need to get some sleep. Early day tomorrow. Food's in the microwave. Goodnight."

My freaking parents are bugged out. Both of them. I locked the bedroom down and grab my duffle bag from the top shelf of the closet. I've been guarding this bag with my life.

I kneel on the floor and dig through my things until I feel the pointy corners of the box. I pull it out and unwrap my shirt I had covering the it. Soon as the time is right, you're going to come in handy. This time I'm not telling a soul, until it's far too late.

It's been a week and a half and I'm just now getting started on my online schooling. Dad showed me the ends and outs about what I was supposed to do. He's getting ready to leave out the door when I say, "When can I get a key?"

"A key? Where are you going without me?"

"Dad!" I whine. "I've been stuck in this house since I got here. I would like to get more fresh air than just stepping out on the balcony. I'm not going to leave the premises."

He hesitates a moment before twirling his spare key from his key ring. "I guess it will be okay, just be careful and don't stroll too far."

I'm so freaking giddy I'm about to burst when he finally closes the door and leaves. I have a laptop and access to the internet! *Yes!*

I click on another tab next to my login page and immediately pull up Facebook to make a new account. Except I can't. It keeps saying page cannot be displayed. *What the freak!* Every social media I can think of gives me the same error. This stupid laptop is broken! I Google something dumb like *why is the sky blue* and guess what? That works! But nothing else does!

I Google what the problem could be and it's saying that someone has blocked the account from all access to those sites and all I needed to do was go into setting and reset the crap. When I do, I'm blocked from even getting to the settings. It says I need admin privileges. When I try to log out and get into the admin account, he has a password set for that too.

I'm hangry (so hungry I'm angry) and tired and that's when I realize I have been searching for the past two hours and now I have a headache. I haven't even gotten my first assignment done.

I get something to eat and then wiz past my assignments like a breeze. Too be honest, I couldn't care less if the crap was right or not. Maybe if I disappoint daddy badly enough with poor grades, he'll feel like a failure and send me back home.

I close the useless laptop and scoop my hair up top into a messy bun. I didn't even brush it. The only person I wanted to look good for wouldn't be seeing me. I pull my hoodie on and slide my feet into my shoes.

As soon as I come out the double doors headed towards the pool area, it felt like the actual sun was only two inches away from me. I felt like SpongeBob in that episode when he went to Sandy's and got dried up like a prune because it was only air and not water. *'Air is not good, Patrick, air is not good.'*

I'm borderline ready to turn around and go back into the apartment because there was no way I was going to take my hoodie off and show my skin with the tank top I had on underneath.

"Omg! Like where did she come from, Alaska?"

"I know right!"

Two girls walk past me, laughing and making fun of me. I didn't know them nor did I care to but there was no way I'm going to let them disrespect me like that.

I walk up to them and deepen my voice a few octaves. "I didn't come from, Alaska but I did come from the hood and I will beat yo ass!" I jerk and they both flinch and fumble over each other to get away from me.

I laugh as they leave me alone because they thought I was this big bad person from the hood. I don't laugh long though because I'm a bit jealous they have each other and I have no one. I miss, Gia's friendship and even, Camila. But I'm missing, Levi the most.

"You're from the hood, huh?"

I look in the direction of the voice and all I see is chocolate abs glistening with water beads. I try to glance into his face but the sun was just a big glare of where his face should be. I didn't try too hard because I didn't give a damn what he looked like. I roll my eyes and walk away.

I sit on one of the nearby lounge chairs and here he comes again. "You're not off to a very good start of making friends, here."

I glance in his direction. "Did I feed you or something? Because I don't remember leaving any milk out or dog bones."

"Oh, I get it. You're calling me a female body part or a female dog." He chuckles. "Well, sweetheart I am definitely not female."

"And I really don't care." I get up annoyed and walk as fast as I can toward the double doors. Until I thought about it. I could use his phone!

I creep back to where the annoying guy sits. "Hi," I sing. "Let's start over..." I hold my hand out for him to shake or whatever.

He stands grabbing his towel in his hand. "No thanks. You only get one chance to make a first impression and you just blew it. Now if you'll excuse me I need to get me a bowl of milk... or a dog bone." He walks away and just leaves me standing there looking hella stupid in my hoodie.

CHAPTER 21
LEVI

"Hi, Liv. How are you?" I asked my mom to call, Nyla's mom to see how, Nyla was doing. I'm still kicking myself for hanging up on her and ignoring her calls.

"I'm good, Nina... and yourself?" My mom and, Nyla's mom exchange pleasantries and I want them to just get to the point. "To what do I owe the pleasure, Nina?"

"Well, we haven't talked in a while and I was just seeing how you and, Nyla were doing."

"Of course, you know, Nyla is with her father."

My mom and I both roll our eyes. I fall back onto my mom's bed next to her listening from speaker phone. "Yes, Liv I know. I was talking

59

about how was she doing so far away and how were you two handling being away from each other."

"I'm not enjoying it, Nina. I wish my baby was still here with me, but I guess I have your son to thank for that."

"How so, Olivia?" I hear the tone change in my mother's voice. It wasn't so cordial anymore.

"I'm not sure you're aware of or even care for that matter, but the last day, Nyla attended James Taylor, Nyla didn't attend. Oh, I dropped her off at school and picked her up, but then I get a call from a recording saying that my daughter was not present to any of her classes. Did you receive the same call about, Levi?"

My mom gives me a mean side eye because she knew that was the day, Nyla and I were together. "I can't say that I recall." *Nice save, mom.*

"It's just as well, I guess. Whatever they *hooked up* to do, it'll never happen again."

My heart saddens again thinking her words might ring true. What if I never see, Nyla again? So, her mom did send her away because of me. I shake my head. She's doing all this to keep her away from me and she's done nothing about, Jax. *She's bogus man!*

I leave my mom to end the call however she wants. I don't really care. I walk into my sister's room. "Gigi can I use your phone?"

"When are you gonna get another one?"

"I don't know. When they can afford to get me one, I guess."

"Well I hope they hurry up." She hands me her phone and I go into my room to call, Camila.

"Hello," She says not sounding as cute as she tried to when I used to call to talk to her.

"Hey, it's, Levi."

"Oh hey, what's up?"

"Nun. You talk to, Nyla lately?"

"Nah, not lately. You got a message or something when I do?"

I couldn't think of anything on the spot besides, "Just tell her I love her and thinking about her."

"Will do. That it?"

"I mean, yea I guess. We kind of ended on a bad note and I'm really hating myself right now."

"Yea, I feel you. She told me."

"She told you? What did she say?"

"Nun much. Just that you got pissed because she had to leave and you hung up on her and wouldn't answer her calls no more."

"Yea, that's pretty much what happened. Does she hate me?"

"She was hurt. We couldn't talk long cause her dad seems strict as shit or something. Not that we girl-talk all like that, anyway. But um, she did tell me that your sister went the hell off on her tho. That's why I wasn't even 'bout to answer this number."

"Whoa, whoa, whoa... what?"

"Yea, she was saying something about she didn't want y'all together in the first place and it was her fault for hurting you and stuff like that."

The more, Camila was telling me about the stuff my sister was saying, the more pissed I got. I couldn't believe Gia would say that. Especially knowing how I feel about, Nyla.

I run to my sister's room and kick her door

open. "So that's what we doin' now, Gigi!" I yell and get close in her face like I wanted to fight her even though I would never lay a hand on my sister.

"Dude, back up!" She tries to push me but it doesn't move me. "What is your problem?"

"You went off on, Nyla? Is that why she's not calling me?"

She crinkles her face and sucks her teeth. "Really, Lee? You come in here going off on me about some chick?"

I bite my lips so hard I can taste the blood coming through from the broken skin. I fight with myself not to tell my sister I hate her right now. "I'm starting to really wish you weren't my sister, right now!"

"All this over a girl who was supposed to be my best friend and who mommy told you to stop talking to anyway?" I get mad and fling her phone at her. "Maybe she not talking to you because she doesn't want to! I didn't say anything to her that didn't need to be said. If someone really wanted to talk to someone, they'd find a way!"

I left out of my sister's room with mixed emotions on her last words. *Which one of us is not trying hard enough to get in touch with the other?*

CHAPTER 22
NYLA

"**N**yla," My dad calls peeking his head inside my guest room. "Can I talk to you for a sec.?"

"Sure dad." Mom usually just burst her way through the door and starts talking. He comes all the way in looking quite dapper. "Where are you off to?"

"That's what I wanted to talk with you about." He seemed nervous. It was weird. "I'm going out to dinner."

"Oh, on a date?" I smile and tease.

"Sorta kinda. We've been seeing each other for a while now."

"So why haven't I met her?"

"That's why I want you to come."

Oh boy! Another one of these dinner reveals. Doesn't anyone in this family just tell news without it having to be in public? "Why don't you just invite her over?"

"Well, we were going over to her house. She's cooking."

"Oh, well, why didn't you just say so." It really wasn't that serious that he was dating someone. I actually found it quite odd and a bit scary that I'd never seen him with or talking about someone.

I get dressed. Nothing too fancy but more presentable than my house shorts and hoodie.

We get on the elevator and it shocks me that we go up instead of down where the lobby is. "Where are we going?"

"I told you. To my lady friend's for dinner."

The elevator dings and we get off and I follow him to a door. "She lives here? In the building?" He nods affirming my questions. Maybe this is where he jogs to on his late-night runs.

"Charlie!" She opens that door like she's so happy to see him. I roll my eyes because I would love to open the door and say, *"Levi!"*

She invites us in and dad makes himself immediately at home. Whereas I sit on the edge of the couch feeling hella uncomfortable.

"Oh!" My dad says like he forgets that I'm here. "Nyla this is Marsha, Shay this is my daughter, Nyla." But he pronounced it Mar'Shay. *Marsha? What old people have the name, Marsha? I bet it's just plain ole, Marsha and she tries to make it sound cool by putting a spin on it. Come to think of it, she doesn't look that old.*

She reaches down and gives me a hug like we're old friends. "Jamie, come out and meet, Charlie's daughter." She yells in the opposite direction.

Great! Was this a set up for me to become friends with her daughter as well? I'd rather not! Just my luck, she'd be one of the girls I had a run in with. I look up and it was much worse.

"No thanks. I'm just going to go into the kitchen and grab a dog bone to dip in my milk."

"Ugh! Seriously?" I roll my eyes and look away from him.

"Am I missing something here?" My dad asks. I didn't say a word. I didn't have a chance to because Mr. Sarcastic answered for me.

"We've met before. I'll just leave it at that."

Awkward silence filled the air as we all sat there with dumbfounded looks on our faces until my dad's lady friend spoke.

"Well, dinner's about ready, shall we sit at the table?"

It was kind of weird because she serves us like we were at a restaurant. First the table was already set and we had salad which was basically plain. Just lettuce, one thin slice of onion, and one grape tomato. There was no shredded cheese, no croutons, and no Ranch in sight... just this tall bottle of brown stuff that sat in the middle of the table.

"Uh, do you have, Ranch dressing?" I couldn't take it anymore, I had to ask. And obviously, Jamie had to laugh like I said something funny.

"Um, no sweetheart... we don't eat, Ranch. I actually make my own ginger salad dressing." She cringed a little like maybe I embarrassed her or maybe she was embarrassed for me. "Just try a little, I think you'll like it."

I contain myself from rolling my eyes and peer over in the bowl next to me. It was some watery brown liquid that had mushrooms sitting in it. I'd rather not say what this brown water looked like. *(You know because people are eating?)* I look at dad because he knows I hate mushrooms. There's no way I'm touching that at all. I think they called it onion soup? *How was that when it had green stuff and mushrooms floating around?*

Back to the salad I go. I pick up the thinly sliced red onion and hold it up to my dad, "do you want this?"

"Sure, honey toss it in," he said referring to his salad bowl.

I take some of the brown clunky stuff and drip a little of it in one spot of my salad. Like literally one piece of lettuce. No way was I going to make the same mistake I did with the pancake syrup. I place the lettuce piece in my mouth praying it wouldn't make me want to vomit. I couldn't believe it! It wasn't bad. I pour a little more on my salad and went to town. That ginger dressing was so good I didn't care anymore that the salad was basically nothing but lettuce! The rest of the meal was the bomb! I thought from the sight of the salad and soup we'd be eating pretty next to nothing for the main course but I was shocked. When she serves the rest of the food, it was like a smorgasbord. We had steak and chicken that was cut up in cubes, shrimp, fried rice, and some kind of Asian noodles. I think I'll be eating over here more often.

CHAPTER 23
LEVI

∽

My keys clink as I grab them up and clutch them in my fist. I'm so pissed right now. I just need to get out of here.

"Where do you think you're going?" She stands in my doorway blocking me. If I really wanted to, I could move her, but I don't because I'm not going to disrespect my mom.

"I'll be back, mom," I say through clenched teeth.

"No, you're not! Give me your keys," she says hands out and ready. She's crazy if she thinks I'm giving up my keys.

"Lee, the worst thing to do is get behind the wheel when you're angry. It's the same thing as driving under the influence."

I bite my lip. "Mom, move!" I try to nudge her a little but not too hard. I just want her to get out of my way and let me get some air.

"If you want to leave and blow off some steam, then take a walk."

I shove my keys into her hand and just like a secret password, she moves aside. I look at her and shake my head as I walk past.

"Lee, I'm sorry okay... where you going? Can I come?" Gia asks trying to keep up with my steps.

"Gigi, leave me alone right now!"

"You never take me with you anymore!" She folds her arms and pout like a baby.

"Grow up, Gia. You can't always go with me!" I yell at her and slam the door.

I take big long strides up the block with no intended destination, just, Nyla on my mind. I hated her mom for making me so pissed at, Nyla right now. *Damn I love that girl.* I would literally marry her right now if I could.

My brain is a jumbled mess. I'm trying to think of ways I can be with her. *How the hell can I make it all the way to, California? Will it be just enough to visit? I'll be eighteen soon, if I have to I'll quit school and just move there. I'll do anything to be with her. Fuck it, I'm just going to have, Gigi call that number she called from. I need to talk to her.*

I'm walking with my hands in my pants pockets because it's a because it's cold as hell. I just have on a hoodie, mom always says to wear a coat, but I ain't doing that especially if it ain't no snow on the ground.

I step off the curb without looking and about piss my pants when I walk up on a car.

"What's up now, bitch? We ain't at school now."

It was, Jax. His hand outstretched from his car window and me staring down at the barrel of his handgun. Matt sat in the passenger seat laughing at how scared shitless I was right now. One pull of the trigger and I would be done for. That's how close I was.

Everything.

Moved.

In. Slow.

Motion.

I haven't even taken a breath yet.

I looked to the right...

Then to the left...

Wondering when my dad was coming to save me.

I look at, Jax's eye which was half closed, still puffy, and red. Now I'm wondering if maybe I shouldn't have done that. Was it worth it? It seemed so at the time. I did it for, Nyla so she could have a break from this asshole. She didn't even come back to school after that.

Maybe this moment was what she kept warning me about.

Now, I'm kind of wishing I had listened.

And I'm wishing mom had listened to me. I could have drove faster than I could run.

Jesus, just let me make it home, I prayed.

I take off running in the opposite direction back to my house.

BANG!

A shot rang out. I never knew a gunshot could be so loud. I never knew I could run so fast. I'm thanking, God that he missed. Maybe it was his bad shooting with only one eye.

BANG!

Another shot.

I should have never left home.

My body jerks and I almost trip and fall, but I regain my balance still running at full speed. My arm burns but I ignore it and keep running.

I feel a bit of comfort as I get closer to my house. I can hear Matt shouting, from the car, "Man enough! What the fuck?" Jax only laughs. They're riding along beside me, taunting me as I run for my life.

I make it to my front door and turn the knob to open it but it's locked. *Great time to finally listen, mom.* "Mom!" I scream and bang on the door that's when I grab my arm and notice the blood. "Moooommm!"

BANG!

Another shot hits me in the back as the front door opens. A few more shots resonate and I see, Gigi. I grab onto her for help to get in the door but she's falling backward herself and I don't know why.

I hear screeching tires as I watch the horror on my mom's face. It's like her eyes are searching and wondering which child to go to. It's a hard decision to make, I know. I try to open my mouth and speak to tell her to see about, Gia but nothing comes out but spews of blood.

I'm choking.

Trying to catch my breath but it feels like I'm

drowning.

I reach out and touch my mom and, Gia. Mom's bent down in the middle between us talking on the phone and telling us both to hold on. Except, I don't know. *I don't think I can, mom.*

I'm trying.

Because if I don't she's going to be mad at me.

I squeeze, Gigi's hand so she can squeeze mind back but she doesn't. She's not moving. *You still can't go with me, Gigi...*

Don't cry, mom.

It's okay.

"Lee! Gia!" My mom cries out as she hangs onto both of us.

I hear sirens in the distance. *Dang mom, I'm sorry to have to make you go out. I know how bad you hate that.*

It's crazy when you get down to a moment like this, I thought about my mom, my dad, and my sister. I didn't think about, Nyla. But the thing I longed for the most, the thing I wanted more than anything... was to breathe.

CHAPTER 24
NYLA

D inner was over and the four of us sat in the living room awkwardly. Neither one of us knowing what to say. I loved my dad, but I felt like I was sitting in a room full of strangers. Even the little conversation that he and his lady friend was awkward because it felt like they didn't want to say too much in front of us.

"I'm going for a walk," Jamison says as he walks to the door.

"Me too." My stomach churns with a burning feeling inside as we walk out into the hallway. "Hey, can I see your phone real quick?" I run up to Jamison and ask.

"What is your obsession with phones and why don't you have one?" He teases but I'm not in the mood.

I snatch the phone from his hand because I don't have time to play games. *Of course, it's locked.* "Put your password in," I say passing him back his phone.

"No. That's why it's a password. To keep unwanted people from getting into it." He starts to walk away as I grab my stomach in pain. "Are you okay?"

"I seriously need a phone." I look into his eyes begging and pleading with mine.

"Fine. Here." He punches in his passcode and hands it to me.

I dial, Camila's number in a hurry. "Camila?"

"Yea."

"Have you talked to Levi or Gia?"

"Not lately, why?"

"Can you please run over there so I can talk to him right quick, please?" I know it was a huge request to ask her to do that for me, but she should be able to get out the house easier than I ever could.

"Seriously? What they got you smokin' on in, Cali?"

OMG! I don't have time for this! Why can't people just do something without all the BS attached to it! I grab my stomach again and wonder where I could retreat to a near bathroom. It feels like I have serious bouts of the bubble guts. "Camila! Please!"

"Fine. If it's that serious, sure I'll get up out of my warm bed, throw some clothes on, *AND A COAT*, because it's cold outside. Not all of us get the luxury of having fun in the sun twenty-four-seven."

I ignore her comment because I don't have time or the energy to respond. I lean back onto the wall for support.

"Is everything, okay?" Jamison asks from the opposite side of the wall.

I wanted to get smart and asks him *if everything looked okay?* But I don't because he is letting me use his phone. "I don't know. I hope so." He stayed on the other side of the wall giving me as much privacy as possible without letting his phone leave his site. "Camila?" I say impatiently.

"What? Damn! I'm walking, it's not across the street you know!" All of a sudden, I couldn't hear her anymore because it was so much noise in the background. "Damnnn!" I barely hear her say.

"Camila, what is that?" I still hear it but I can hear her better now.

"A whole bunch of ambulances, firetrucks, and police cars just zoomed down the street passing me."

I groan into the phone. "Where are they going?" I clinch my stomach again because I was not having a good feeling about this.

"I don't know, Nyla... they just zoomed past me."

"Well run, make sure it isn't, Levi's."

Camila sucks her teeth, "now you just asking for too much." I hear her huff and puff for a few seconds. "Oh my gosh! Oh, my go... Nyla!"

"What! What is it? Is it, Levi?"

"I-I don't know. Police is everywhere! They bringing out two people, I can't see who..."

I don't need to know who, I just know that one of them is, Levi.

Blackness...

CHAPTER 25

∽

"**H**ello?" A strange voice summons, Camila from the other side.

"Yes, who the hell is this and where is, Nyla?" Camila stands on the corner watching things unfold from the Nash residence as the cold whips at her ankles.

"This is, Jamie. She was using my phone, she just passed out, I have to get her father." The line goes dead as, Camila stares at it and then stuffs it into her coat pocket.

"What the hell is going on!" She yells into the cold air as her breath comes out resembling cigarette smoke. From the distance she spots, Levi's mom standing between two ambulances covered in blood. Her heart sinks as she had no idea what to do. Her first thought was to run home and get, Nyla's mom but she knew she didn't have time for that. Camila takes off running through the crowd to get to, Levi's mom.

"Mrs. Nash!" Camila shouts as she runs up to her and throws her arms around the strange woman. "I'm, Nyla's sister." She introduces herself and the woman's face lightens as best it could in a time like this.

"My kids! My babies!" Was all she could shout.

"We need to move now!" Someone shouts from one of the ambulances.

Nina is a bundle of nerves not knowing which ambulance to jump into. How could she choose one child over the other?

"Mrs. Nash, Levi and I are close. I'll ride with him that way you can ride in the other one."

Nina was grateful for the young girl as she runs to, Gia's ambulance and hop inside. Camila did the same.

Camila tries her best to stay out of the way while the paramedics work on, Levi. She reaches out and touches his ankle. "You okay, bro. Please hang in there." She didn't know what else to say. She didn't know if he was going to be okay, she didn't even know if he was still breathing. All she knew was there was a lot of blood.

Camila whips out her phone and dials, Olivia. "Livia?"

"I can't talk right now, I'm on the other line with, Charles, he says, Nyla past out, and he's on his way to the hospital with her. I need to give him her info."

"I know that's why I was calling, plus I'm on the

way to the hospital too, I'm in the ambulance."

"Ambulance? Why?"

"Something bad happened to Levi and his sister."

"Bad like what?" Olivia's voice takes on a new tone of urgency.

"I think they got shot."

"Shot! Both of them?"

"Yea, I think." At least that was the bits and pieces that, Camila picked up.

"I'll be there as soon as I'm done with, Charles. Nina must be a nervous wreck. Where's Eli?"

Camila hadn't the slightest idea who, Eli was, but she took a best guest that it was, Levi's dad. "Uh, I don't know. It was just his mom when I got here."

"I'll have to find his number and give him a call. I need to go."

At the hospital, Camila sat holding, Nina's hand in silence until Eli showed up. Camila backed away down the hall to give the parents some privacy, but close enough that she could see what was going on.

Her phone rings displaying a familiar number she hadn't saved into her phone yet. "Nyla?"

"Um... Jamie."

"Oh. How's my sister?"

"She's fine, I guess. I mean it's not life threatening or anything. They're in there now talking to her."

"That's good."

"So how are things on your end? It sounded pretty intense earlier."

"Oh, it's still intense. Just without all the blaring sirens."

"I hope it all ends well."

"Thanks. I'm actually glad you called. Even though I don't know you, it kind of brings my heart rate down a few notches."

"Well, I'm glad I could be of help. If we're being honest, I'm glad to be talking to you as well because hospitals can be tedious."

CHAPTER 26
NYLA

❝Let me see your phone!" I yell at my dad who's looking at me like I need to be in a strait jacket. *Yea, I'm going crazy because they're making me that way. It's a freaking phone! I can't get pregnant through the damn thing!*

The doctor comes in to tries to calm me down. "You're going to need to calm down." She says looking into my eyes trying to get on my level. It works for a second but then I think about, Levi and I just want to use a phone to check on him. I yell and scream for no apparent reason.

"What the hell is wrong with her?" My dad says to the doctor. "Can't you give her something to calm her down?"

"You mean like a sedative?" The doctor says back.

"Yeah, I guess."

The doctor shakes her head, "can't in her condition."

"What kind of condition does she have?" My dad asks now worried.

The doctor fiddles around on the tiny laptop. "According to her blood work, she has elevated levels of HCG."

"What does that mean?" My dad asks as his lady friend's mouth drops and she grabs onto him.

"That should make her about four weeks pregnant. We're waiting for an ultrasound technician so we can get an ultrasound to make sure everything okay." The doc turns to me. "That's probably why you passed out. And you're a little dehydrated. You need more fluids.

"I drink stuff," I say feeling calmer that my plan had worked. I was going to wait a few more days before I used the pregnancy test hid away in my duffle bag to be sure. But I guess I don't need to know. I smirk.

"I'm sure you do, but I'm talking about water, young lady." *I like her. She's nice.*

"Okay. I can do that." I smile.

"I know you can." She pats my hand. "I'll be back in a little bit to check on you."

My dad couldn't wait until the doctor left out. "So, your crazy bitch of a mother sent you to me knowing you were pregnant?"

"Honey. Honey, calm down." His lady friend tries to calm him in the way the nurse did me. "She's so early, I'm sure her mother had no idea."

My dad jumps up and paces back and forth. "Nope. No way a daughter of mine is going to have a baby at sixteen. You're getting rid of it." He points his finger at me.

"No. I'm not. I did that last year, no way I'm doing it again. Especially with this one." I say nonchalantly.

"Did what last year?" My dad looks me up and down like he wanted to fight.

"Abortion dad. I got pregnant in the ninth grade and mom made me abort it. I'm not doing it again. I don't care what you say."

His lady friend had a look on her face that said this was too much for her to deal with at their level in the relationship.

"Oh, and since we're sharing. I got raped a few months back too."

"What!?" My dad looked like he was going to explode but I didn't care. "Why the hell didn't your mother think that information wasn't important enough to let me know?" *Wait until he finds out nothing even happened to the guy who did it.* "Is this how you got pregnant?"

"Honey. She said a few months ago, she's only four weeks..."

He looked down at his Marsha, "Shut up!" His voice raspy as his mouth hung open wide and his eyes were bugged. "I feel like, I paid all this money for my dream car and it's a lemon!"

"Ouch, dad. That stung a bit. Can I go home now? Like home, home with mom?"

My dad slams the door on his way out ignoring my question.

CHAPTER 27

C harles whizzes past, Jamison who's still talking on the phone with, Camila and into a secluded stairwell.

Before, Olivia can say, hello, Charles began to speak. "What the fuck did you send me, Liv!"

"Excuse me? That reference had better not be used towards my child."

"Yea, well I'm sending your child right the hell back to you!"

"Oh no you're not! I'm about to walk into the hospital right now to see this boy she's in love with and her best friend." Olivia takes a deep breath. "Charles, I don't know if they're dead or alive. It could have been our baby!" Oliva is sincere and feels bad for the way she'd treated, Levi lately.

"Yeah, well... our baby is about to have a baby, Liv and I can't deal with that."

Olivia stopped dead in her tracks as her heart sank. "Come again?"

"You heard me, Liv. Now I'm really sorry about whatever is going on there, but this is your shit you made with her. I'm not about to clean it up. You sent her to me about five weeks to damn late."

"She's five weeks?"

"Four."

Olivia did a quick mental calculation and she knew exactly when that might have happened. "Seems like I was twenty-four hours late. *Damn!*"

"I don't give a damn how late, Liv. The problem is she's late for her female shit. What are we going to do?"

"Hmm..." Olivia twisted her lips. "I'm already pregnant, Charles. I can't deal with this. This time it's on you! I'll support whatever you decide, but, Nyla is not coming home. We may have just save her life."

Jamison took the phone in to, Nyla so she could talk to, Camila.

"Hey sissy, how are you?" Camila sings softly into the phone.

"I'd be better if I knew what was going on."

Camila sighs heavily not wanting, Nyla to be worried and freaked out. "I don't know anything yet."

"Who was it?"

"Levi and Gia."

"What?" Nyla shouts into the phone. "What happened?"

"I don't know, Nyla."

"Tell me why they're both in the hospital, Camila!"

"Nyla, all I know is they got shot."

"Both!?"

"Yea." Camila's stomach hurt wondering if she should have given, Nyla that much information.

"Do they know who did it?"

"I don't know."

"We both know who it was!"

Camila knew just as well as Nyla that it was, Jax.

A blood curdling scream lets out and rings throughout the hallway and through the receiver into, Nyla's ears.

"Who is that?" Nyla asks.

Camila heart thumps wildly as she watches, Nina continues to scream onto the cold linoleum floor. Eli bends down trying to console her even though he was breaking as well.

"Oh no. Oh my gosh." Camila says as she tries to read the doctors lips from afar.

"Who's screaming?" Nyla asks again feeling helpless that she was so many miles away.

"Levi's mom," Camila says slightly inaudible.

"Why's she screaming? What happened, Camila!"

"I-I don't know."

OTHER READS BY HEAVEN J. FOX

Kissing Cousins – YA Fiction (Short Story)
Kissing My Best Friend's Brother – YA Fiction
Series
Kissing Cousins – Audiobook

<u>The Westbrook High Series</u>
Fitting In (Is Hard to Do (Semester I) Book I – YA
Fiction
Fitting In (Is Hard to Do (Semester II) Book II – YA
Fiction
Summer '16: Fitting In (Is Hard to Do) Book III –
YA Fiction

<u>Standalones</u>
Something Worth Fighting For – (Christian
Fiction)